STELLA MARIS AND OTHER KEY WEST STORIES

Stella Maris

& Other Key West Stories

Michael Carroll

TURTLE POINT PRESS *Brooklyn, New York*

Requests for permission to make copies of any
part of the work should be sent to:
Turtle Point Press
208 Java Street, Fifth Floor
Brooklyn, NY 11222
info@turtlepointpress.com

Library of Congress Cataloging-in-Publication Data is
available from the publisher upon request.

An early version of "Key West Funeral" appeared in Speak My
Language edited by Torsten Højer, Little, Brown, 2015.

Design by Alban Fischer Design

Paperback ISBN: 978-1-885983-68-8
Ebook ISBN: 978-1-885983-69-5

Printed in the United States of America

To Patrick Ryan,
for the voyage out

Philosophy that comes down from the heavens is the kind that—from Plato to Levinas by way of Kant and Christianity—needs a world behind the scenes to understand, explain, and justify this world. The other line of force rises from the earth because it is satisfied with the given world, which is already so much.

—MICHEL ONFRAY

Contents

Sugar and Gold

I'VE LOST NOT a few, he thought, humorously noting the unlikeliness of this syntax in actual human thought—while a group of four young cuties, naked by the pool except for their striped towels, drank and complained. Their mostly educated, nasal voices wobbled under the shade of their umbrella:

"I just think, *Why am I here?* I plunked down a grand for this *gay cruise* and already I'm thinking, *I'm on said boat and there's no one here for me?* I go on Grindr, and—*nobody*. Nada."

"Okay. A? *Nada* means 'nothing.'"

"Exactly."

"And B? Look. At. This glorious day."

"That was long and drawn-out."

"Right?"

"*Everybody on this ship is ancient,* I'm thinking. Like, Code of Hammurabi decrepit."

"Well, now you're off the boat for a few hours and you're here with us. We're not bad!"

"I know, right?" the third one said further.

The fourth had not said anything in a while but sat up and noted, "I think it's all right for male couples from the First Babylonian Dynasty to join the middle-age-and-under crowd."

"Just because that's what *you* like."

An older guy at the bar with his back to them was listening, drinking his vodka: *Well, that's me they're talking about.*

Sex could be beautiful, or just great, or at least good or acceptable, yet so many in his generation and under had died.

Earlier the older guy had been invited to eat out the asshole of a thirty-something and had done it and taken his time savoring the sweet beige stink of the anus between the owner's pair of loose buns. The whole thing had happened in the video room upstairs, the kid prone on a carpeted dais cursing the guy, Dale, and asking him if it tasted good. Yet for decades Dale had been turned off by the idea (he'd been married all along and thought that's what did it; the thought of kissing his wife after doing that), but an hour or so ago the offer had been irresistible. The younger guy was cute but not incredibly hot, and the offer (extended by the kid's older lover, who'd watched) gave Dale a thrill. And the taste of the hole had given him wood, not a lot but enough sap to make the branch grow. That, the kid's imperfect cuteness and rubbery cheeks, the filthily straightforward manner in which the lover had asked him to do the rimming, and the fact that there was someone else watching, all of them taking their towels off. Dale had licked, slurped, played with himself.

Then come out poolside for a drink at the bar, aware of being casually watched, but not by the four younger men under the umbrella kicking up the subtropical calm with their laughter.

Nearby, a sixth guy—the one making these observations—the self-described writer, although no one here would know his name, thought: *If this is the end of civilization, I would not exit it.*

He'd started drinking early and had lost temporarily the daily will to write his sentences.

It's the perfect place.

The bartenders and barbacks were from elsewhere.

They were from Eastern Europe and beyond. That meant Georgia and Kazakhstan. They had to put up with these queers, as they, the workers, were mostly heterosexual. You might never penetrate their professional demeanors or get to the hearts of their desires. They didn't deny desire, they were downright sweet; wink at them and they'd blush. In halting English, they'd attempt to make a joke or pun, but the attempts were off-tone, missing a nuance. Their apparent awkwardness only made them more adorable. They had a job to do, and papers here in America to maintain.

The real Americans were foreign, wanting citizenship so bad, and you wondered why.

You knew why, but still.

The native-born Americans were spoiled, wanting to be waited on in the polite way of the foreigners.

And I remember being too young to understand almost anything but the idea, which I didn't get, that Jesus had died for me—and what did that mean? Died for me why, how? I mean, how does anyone die for someone else if not in person, as in a prisoner trade-off? Absurd, and if you think about it, unnecessary.

There was a moment coming out of the baptismal whatchamahoozie, the tank in front of a congregation, chlorine-smelling, when you asked yourself, *What was that all about?* Died for me?

Easier to see that now, when you imagined a lover. You'd die for that man, sure. He was a physical piece of evidence of your heart and life. He'd saved you already, which was the thing.

You'd fight even after he was gone and you were still angry, although your thoughts were tender.

And he was in a restaurant now and there was a couple, you just knew how they'd voted.

The woman with her platinumed hair looked at him and said, "We just got off the ship!"

He said, "Where y'all from?" Because that's what you asked strangers here.

The jagged desire to extend hospitality had begun to chafe and scrape inside him. His mother, for instance, was a moron. She, too, was going to make America great again.

"Ohio."

The Ohioans really took up the rear stopping off from cruises down here.

He was drinking his tequila, just finishing his dinner. He wouldn't engage.

He said, "I have a theory. Every American has done time in either Texas or Ohio, once."

"Done time?" the woman said.

The husband shook his head slowly and tightly.

The country was at war morally, still, and it was going to be at war for a good while.

Once the Hollywood line went, "I have only one quarrel with you. This ends tonight." But this was before the big faux-billionaire asshole had come in swinging the wrecking ball.

The divisions had deepened. You could retreat into your homosexual redoubts. Gay guesthouse or late-night bar that still allowed smoking and didn't close until four a.m. But then you crawled out before the light came up, drag queens flirting with the husbands and teasing the wives. All in good fun, but it wasn't fun because the grave of America was still fresh, the democratic dream all over. He was one of those, too, who'd grown up using the n-word. He wasn't shocked that he'd ever been this way, but it was a disappointment in retrospect. How many years of friendship and loving might he have missed out on? (Anyway, he was glad he was gay. You could find some love inside the space of twenty minutes. *One, I'm done*).

In this clothing-optional gay guesthouse compound, he heard such stories, neck-snapping ones.

"Back in my arsehole town," the Scot said, "my mother when I was seventeen said to me, after she found out, 'A murderer or a thief or a child molester, that I could explain. But how do I explain you? No.' So I packed my kit, I hit out for London, I never looked back, I didn't have to so I didn't. So I understand what you're saying, you just cut out your whole entire family. And I was thinking, *I'm about to do the same.* The last argument I had with my mom—I thought that."

The vulgarity of *being,* of understanding oneself. *This is what I like. It's who I am.*

He remembered being repulsed by his own body, while being so excited by it.

They looked around the pool area, from under the shade of the bar shed.

The Scot said, "That guy's shorts, his arse is like two rabbits fighting in a cloth sack."

"He's pretty perfect."

"Oh, he's more than perfect. And he came down the stairs from the sunning area just now while you were in the gents', and just like you said, the reason he complimented my tattoo was to talk to me, like a conversation starter. He just comes right out and admits that!"

"Like I told you."

"And right you were! He wants to come back to my room with me."

"You're welcome."

"Thank you is right."

The Scot, Gregory, was drinking a Tara Reid, and said, "I'm living on sugar and alcohol."

"What's in it?"

"About forty thousand liquors and some juice and I don't know what all. It'll get you fucked in under an hour, just the one Tara Reid."

"Who is Tara Reid?"

"A disgraced television personality, or maybe not disgraced but tragic."

"I predict that you'll go over to that guy and say something not necessarily suave, just as a conversation opener, and then—"

"No, it's already done. We're meeting in my room in fifteen minutes."

"My work here is finished. I have to go to a dinner party. Wish I could stay, and hear."

"Night, love."

"Night."

THE DINNER PARTY is by a rich older couple who are fun and liberal and worried about America.

The rich wife has just asked her husband to tell his story about the Walgreens cashier.

He says, "I said to her 'How long have I been coming here?'"

"And what did she say?" says another guest.

"She didn't say anything. She looked at me like I was insane. Which I am, admittedly."

The view is incredible, at a lookout point where the Atlantic meets the Gulf of Mexico. And it's sunset. There are clouds, they're on fire. The party's having dinner on an expansive stone deck. And he's so drunk that he's content again. He's stopped thinking about his mother, his mother. God, that woman, the deplorables, who knew?

The wind from a confluence of weathers is kicking up and streaking the palms diagonally and he thinks, *I shouldn't be so negative. Social media is telling me not to focus on negativity.*

He would drown her, he would—he'd strangle and kick her.

The bleeding sky, and just under it the sea. It's a

silvery-green swelling, roiling, the smell is fresh and saline—less of the halide, farty, sewer smell. The freshness makes him want to fuck.

I don't have to feel this way, he thinks. *I can forget her. The way I've forgotten lovers.*

I can call them up when I need to, but when I call her up, nothing. Blind white rage.

Later he's downtown at the back bar drinking tequila. There's an enclosed patio and he's fucked there before. The tourists mill by on the other side of a tall fence. On the patio there is a couch and some chairs around it. Guys pull out their dicks. Sometimes women are in the crowd, they watch. This turns him on, anything public. It's his shame writ large. It wants him exposed. It wants him. The disgust, the excitement. It all goes together, in the old gay custom.

The queer. Making it more delicious. He's delicious in that moment. He rocks, is hot.

But he's not on the patio. He's inside drinking tequila and soda with limes.

The younger man is explaining his job as a merchant marine.

"It's a hundred and thirteen feet long. Wait, let me show you a video? The most difficult is going through the Poe Lock. If shipping were suddenly closed on the Great Lakes, well forty percent of the American economy would be fucked, like instantly fucked. I pilot that freighter. I have two and a half feet on either side. It's a frigging gas, it's almost like sex. You like sex?"

"I used to."

"What does that even *mean*?"

"Kidding, of course."

"Right? You get basically two and a half feet on either side in the Poe Lock—"

Sped-up, the video was impressive. The freighter pushed on slowly, the passage narrow.

He asked if the kid had ever heard the song "The Wreck of the *Edmund Fitzgerald*."

He used to try that one at karaoke.

"Heard of it? Whenever it comes on we immediately turn it off. Bad luck."

"I heard sailors are superstitious."

"You don't even know the half of it. Like, looking at you now, I'm getting your energy."

"Is it bad?"

"It's not that great. You seem like someone who—"

"Who what?"

"Never mind."

THEY USED TO go to the beach on a weekday. His father had gone to work and his brother was off at school. He went into her room when she was still in bed, sleeping it off, and got into bed with her, and they snuggled. It was all so harmless, he'd thought. They just needed each other.

He said, "I'm sick," and she didn't say anything, just made room for him on the bed.

They were intimate and warm, snuggling. But he thought, *I can't tell her anything.*

They stopped at McDonald's, ate it on the way. They were listening to the radio singing.

He was the boss. He turned the radio up. She let him be the boss.

She said, "You're very adult. You're mature for your age."

She was Southern and pronounced it *mah-TOOR*.

An idiot, he now thinks.

How could you go from such needy intimate love to blind-rage hatred, kill-her hatred?

It was in that pronunciation. *Mah-TOOR.*

She'd wanted to go to college, but her father had said she'd have to live at home.

Then she eloped.

Were he still talking to her he'd say, "If only you'd gone to college and not married."

His father was dead. His anger should have been directed at the man who was now dead.

Or both.

"You let him run all over you. I hate you for that. I hate you for that. I hate you for it."

※ ※ ※

THE WIFE OF the rich couple calls quite unexpectedly.

She says, "I wanted to ask you something."

"Sure."

"It's really beyond the call of duty."

"Ask away, Penny."

She was self-deprecating to a frustrating degree. Maybe she liked him because he tried to draw out the straight shooter in her. He tried to keep her laughing when they were alone together, though he sometimes got too drunk to make sense with his jokes and his puns.

"Well, it's just this—and again I know it's a lot to ask—and you know me, I hate to sound needy or ask for anything ever—I value your time—but—"

"Penelope, please. Anything. You and Stu have both been unbelievably generous."

"Well, darn then, I'll just come out and say, ha-ha, what's on my mind! Stewie and I are having our big anniversary this summer and I was wondering if you could just come up and stay with us in the house on Cape Cod and just help us with little things. Nothing too tremendous—I promise, it won't be like that New Year's in Palm Beach. That was too much. That was—"

"No, not too much at all. It was just that I don't have experience with party planning."

"That was all my fault. Stewie got sore with me for weeks and weeks. But nobody who knows us expects us to be the Duke and Duchess of Windsor. I just need—to lean on someone?"

"My favorite thing. I always enjoy your company and your household menagerie."

"Ha-ha, you said menagerie!"

Good, he thought, I can sleep and eat for free and be in a beautiful place all summer.

He was broke, and alone now, so it was perfect.

"GREGORY WE SORT of lost last night. We all went to dinner downtown—then we said good-bye to him. And then this morning I saw him carrying a coffee back to his room. Apparently he had woken up on some stranger's porch without his wallet and slunk back here. I felt bad for him."

This was the long cool drink of water who worked for the State Department.

Poker-faced, he said, "Do you think it was the Deep State?" with a wet, sibilant ending.

"I think it was the Tara Reids."

"Is he okay?"

"I think he's taking the divorce a little harder than he expected."

There were several sudden singles going through a divorce, including this one, the long cool drink of water whose name he couldn't remember. Absolute beauties, unicorns such as the long cool drink of water, scared the shit out of him. He could compliment them a little, but he'd never touch. He wouldn't, like Gregory, who made fun of himself for his weight, just go over to the canal pilot's ex-husband and start talking to him: this Ryan sunning, and next thing you knew they were in bed.

But still, he was able to ask Ryan, "Are you having fun? Hooking up?"

"A little. I'm basically just here to relax after the divorce."

Weirdly happening at the same time: the new asshole president and these gay divorces.

And there was Ryan's ex, the merchant marine who'd already planned to come down with his hubs before the divorce, and paid for everything, and they'd decided not to cancel, just be civil and go ahead with it. They were divorcing but wanted to be grownups, and fuck Trump.

"Are you okay?" he asked when he saw the merchant marine in the outdoor hot tub.

"A little tense."

"Because of your ex?"

"Yes."

"Is he jealous?"

"Unbelievably."

"Was it mutual?"

"I fucked up. I violated the rules. I did some very bad things and I'm sorry and all and I wish I hadn't done them, but I did them, and there's nothing I can ever do to make it up to Chet."

"How's he, all right now?"

"Pissy. I just went a little crazy in the last year after the election. They kept talking about budget cuts, and it hasn't been the best time to be out. Maybe I was trying to sabotage us?"

He wanted to get the chlorine off himself and he went to shower. Naked Sunday was all in swing and the indoor hot tub in the wet areas was full of simmering men holding their drinks, a little woozily, or else with dignity as they sat about with their genitals bobbing underwater. At the showers one man was bent over holding on to the grab bars grunting while another grasped his hips and fucked away at him. There were three showerheads erupting full-spray, but not *their* showerheads—and he thought, *How wasteful.* Then he remembered he had his glasses on. He was a middle-aged guy with some beef and pudge projecting and hanging here and there, and all he wanted to do once the top had disengaged was ratchet himself in. Wearing glasses, ridiculous.

Driving out to the beach after McDonald's, they were listening to "Lunching to the Oldies." He remembered wishing she'd just divorce his father. It was a feeling of anxious peace, this holding pattern of skipping school and being naughty, and maybe that would be part of his anger later. (You hung on to things bent over, emotional grab bars while life pummeled away at you.)

"I heard this at prom," she'd said.

His parents had met in seventh grade and dated on and off until graduation. His father had gone off to UT Knoxville. Been kicked out after too many fraternity shenanigans, shipped home to enroll in a Catholic college in Memphis, and they'd suddenly eloped to Bryson City in the Smokies. Started having babies too fast. That was the menace, too young, too dumb.

It was "Brown Eyed Girl."

He'd said, "Did you know right away that you loved him?"

"Yes, God yes. But no. I wanted to play the field, meet boys. I was living in downtown Memphis with my girl-friends, doing the books for a dentist, and this dental student Kirby caught my eye. Asked me out. Had a few dates with me, nothing serious. We'd petted but I think I was just getting away from my father. Your granddaddy didn't want me going to college unless I lived at home, and I was like *Nuh-uh*. That's not college. That's just more of the same."

"But why Dad then?"

"He came home. And I told him what had happened. Kirby drove me out to the Bluffs, the Chickasaw Bluffs—at first nothing serious, to my mind. He drove us right up to the Bluffs in a T-Bird his daddy had bought him, baby-blue with the portholes. I'd thought all along it was the kind of car a guy who was kind of fruity would drive. Baby blue. He said, 'I'm going to drive us straight over and off if you don't agree to marry me.' I screamed, 'Yes, yes! I'll marry you.' And when he got me home on Germantown Road I got out of there straight fast, went running in to my daddy crying. And my daddy called your daddy, who came over, and he and I talked a time. Then we snuck out one night, flat eloped . . ."

Everybody was moving up, taking out the ain'ts and cain'ts from their talking.

It would have been: Kennedy and the assassination, then more assassinations. Johnson and Vietnam (his father had a 3-A deferment from having a family and going to college), then the protests, etc., Nixon and Watergate. The oil crisis. Carter, so hated by Southerners. Reagan and a sense of renewal or something but in reality just more greed and tax-cut talk. Then AIDS and the mind-wipe of the eighties and early nineties. The hiding and jumping out of the closet, awkward.

Which took him up to Craig, and they'd been together for twenty-two years.

Craig had walked out on a beautiful morning. They'd not slept together in years. He was in truth ready to deal with that as a reality taking him up to old age and death just for the security of it. He'd gotten half of everything, a real divorce after a legal marriage, another renewal of one not completely loveless. Love was like that. It was hanging in, through disease and bankruptcy. And then it was nothing. Life worked that way.

Half of everything was somehow plenty.

Then in the fullness of time it was practically nothing.

Primal Recognition

(to Ann Beattie)

DO YOU WANT to get on the good foot? Need to be assigned a red line just to stay within your boundaries? Are you able to ask others to stay within theirs? Do you have the stuff? Can you come up to snuff? What are you made of? And, oh heaven, are you able to break it all down to its constituent parts; and what are those? Can you stay in love sufficient to the cause? Is your general affection of a non–New Age variety, while disposing of tribal Judeo-Christian notions?

Are you—at the age of fifty—still wildly horny, with or without the aid of a hard-on pill?

Am I, well, up to snuff?

Are you on any other medications, prophylactic or otherwise?

Do I get in step, go on PrEP?

The boys these days are for skin on skin, flesh up inside another's flesh. An outrage, a blessing.

They want to be able to assume, and Rick has been hesitating, although he longs for those old days. Gene used to say Rick's verse reminded him of cruising for tricks in the old days.

"The quick exchanges between guys, almost like signs or advertisements. Terse words."

This was shortly before Gene's succumbing. Once Key West had meant freedom to Rick, but now it was a chaining-to: *Coral rocks / under pirate nights / slice-moon and ragged cloud / passing over / nudged by sticky salty wind, / And time. Like Saturn, / eating the young / prancing past, / as fast food / as pick-up / or delivery / for bulimic gods. / Prometheus housebound.*

Gene had gone to the hospital and never come home. Transferred to a hospice-prison, VA dime. Vietnam had not hurt Gene's body, had barely scratched his spirit—rather, fortifying Gene's cheer. He'd hit the ground boots-first from the tongue-out maw of a C-130. Taken his discharge to New York, found a roach trap on Horatio, lived a life. Worked at a magazine, cut his teeth, and was there at Stonewall. Author of a dozen collections. Subject of articles, studies, a biography. Had even sort of pushed the dark extents of his coming-out agonies. Had always been loved and for a long time remained physically enticing. Had the puzzlingly perennial body of "youth," was a top, avoided

AIDS, lost every lover until the deep eighties. Cried and gotten back up and gone to all the funerals, memorialized, spoken, risen back. Kicked drugs, booze, and cigarettes, was called the Slim Reaper. Only lines in his face, with monochrome author portraits like eternal acid etchings, happy, serious, derided, surviving. Until he began to forget things and then began to forget everything, his name, the president's, his daily medications, his profession.

And was ending here, where the care was not so good yet the transfer back up north Rick could not countenance. The road trip with a babbler. Or the flight with a seat-shitting passenger.

Rick had caught Gene in the mid-nineties in London, where Gene was enjoying discovery by the English. A host of hosts, parties everywhere that warm summer, unharassed except by the lightest of rains. Gene was prize-heaped; he laughed at every new honor, a laugh so frequent and so bemusing it subsided into grief-chuckles. Rick had pointed this out—they shared everything and were mostly always honest—and Gene had liked it, calling his next collection *Grief-Chuckles* and dedicating it to Rick. It was supposed to go on, and seemed like it would forever go on.

When finally Rick had published his own first collection, he'd called it *The New Terse*.

Rick rarely picked up his cell. In the last days of lively, conscious, shared love between them, Gene had decided

Rick's drag name should be Mist McCalling. Gene could be fun, but wit was not his long suit. He was only unfrivolous on the page. Gene was a delight in a crowd or at a gathering, but his poems were hammeringly serious; at times hot-angry. He used one image or metaphor, then cut it into pieces and inserted hunks of bloody lamb, shards of the cross, cooling wedges of the Sunday-dinner apple pie in Greenville, 1959. It was his Southern charm, they said. It was all the things his readers and arch critics said, but it was ice-harsh, ladle-drafts of pain dipped up out of the beech-stand well, splashed into the surprised, grateful mouth before the hike home, and it was mystified confusion of the self, the farmhand that had dared, the farmhand's wife that didn't tell, the sister that had told. It was hell and adolescent mortification, a sense of condemnation, forgiveness wrapped in a sibilant hush, awareness of some God but no longer the Hebraic one, questioning, his early lowball achievement at school soothsaying abject failure.

Gene was beyond calling now. Rick was beyond being in touch with others. He set his phone to vibrate and biked up to Stock Island to the facility. His days were this. Keeping up with the bills and expenses, accounting. Waking up sober when he could (he should get clean), visiting.

They knew him and nodded as he took off his biking helmet.

Gene had a new roommate, a ginger man watching

his overhead TV who said, as Rick was entering, "Can I have my life back? Not all of it, just the part you stole, you fucking troll."

"Sure," said Rick. "I'll be right back with it, promise."

The patient whimpered and his whimper faded.

The man was young, his most startling feature. He looked like an actor from an Iraq War movie, and had been to Iraq. Iraq wasn't his problem, exactly. He might have developed what he had with or without the war. The disease had presented in the fourth decade. Rick understood this to be a little early, but they were still finding out things about chemicals that had been used over there, their side effects and more permanent effects. One side effect or development of the disease was the patient's talking to the air, giggling, the giggling subsiding into private grievings.

"Just the part you stole, not the rest of it, you son of a—" and choked it off and sneered.

Something about the young man, whose name was Brian, made Rick a little happier. Of course a tragic lightness, in musing. Occasionally when he spoke he sounded like Peter Finch in *Network*, bemused, strident. But when he whimpered, Brian was a boy, a relative youth. For a moment each visit here and there, totaling no more than five minutes, Rick felt horrible. Brian otherwise lay looking innocent, hands up like paddles—and then he was tolerable, quite sweet.

Rick toed around the curtain to see Gene, who brightened blankly and said, "Hey!"

There was never any evidence that Gene recognized Rick. Gene started talking, too.

Gene said, "Hi, angel. I was just talking to Susie and she said you'd have that reaction."

"What reaction?"

Brian said, "Have you seen Joe? He's been redeployed! I just missed him, actually."

Gene said, "Oh I wish she'd just shut up."

There was a time when things were funny, but now the funny was just too weird. It was all a neurological glitch, the laughter around here. An automatic, allergic social reaction.

Gene said, "I remember when I hit my head on a root, a hard root. And I think that was the source of all this problem. It was all a mistake. Can you explain that to them? Can we go? It was an accident, and I'd like—if you could just tell them—I'd like to go now."

Rick said, "I would love that very much, darling. Do you want me to call the doctor?"

"Is there a doctor here?"

"We're in a hospital."

"No, we're not. We're back at Clay Mountain. Right after I got home from the infirmary with measles. My mother said, 'It's the kind of night to build a fire.' Can we build a fire?"

"I wish we could, darling, but there's no fireplace here."

"Where are we?"

"We're at the hospital. No fireplaces here."

"Shit. I wish we were back at Clay Mountain. Then we could roast a pig. Yum yum!"

"Is that where you hit your head on the root, Gene?"

"No, no!" Gene groaned as though insulted. "Back at Dak To near the border with Laos."

Gene was no longer a part of Rick's life, and Rick's life was attenuated outside of the hospital. Gene was a few steps from gone, and Rick was in pain but only for a couple of hours each day. He counted those hours but only while he was visiting, leaving when Gene fell asleep watching TV.

When he would leave, Gene sleeping with reality TV turned down, Rick crept backward, despising himself, not cursing life or his life, merely wishing he were stronger, or something.

Brian was awake and said, "I had a boyfriend. Have you seen Joe? Is Joe dead, too?"

HE BICYCLED TOWARD a spectacular sunset. This had to be a poem, a moment, this circumstance.

Leaving you, / having, almost, / been you . . .

The days were longer here than up north. So close to the tropical zone. The canals were like twisted ways of water and mangrove. This, too, would have to go in—marrying Vietnam and their lives together later and lately. He biked over the causeway and thought he saw a red iguana deciding to call it a day and crawling into the brush. The stand-up paddleboarders were all gone, heading to the tourists' seafood restaurants. You had to love the ocean to vacation here. It would be difficult for him to leave, even after Gene was gone. It had almost gotten too late to leave. New York had receded into this penumbra of impossibility, of impenetrability, and the rent would be ridiculous. He might even leave his small storage unit in Queens full and sleeping, like a tomb housing the nineties and early aughts. How could he even hope to return to it, unlock it? The truth was, he had things in both New York and Key West to return to, but Key West won.

Ivan was there. As he locked his bike on the side of the cottage, he heard rumbling within. Ivan was making chili. Once he'd presented a stew made from an iguana, a recipe he'd gotten from a Nicaraguan working in the same restaurant. Rick still hadn't given him the key, thinking perhaps Gene would come home again, that a miracle trial would revive him. There was talk of one, the miracle drug that already was exhibiting success dissolving and eradicating the choking proteins that slouched on and smothered the neurons, defying the vital electrical signals, so he'd read, but it was too late for Gene. Clinical trials were for earlier on in the onset of symptoms, which Gene had been having for five years or so. Recently Ivan had brought Rick's appetite back, but not for iguana.

Jorge says / with iguana broth / Gene will heal.

This generation, they would say anything to anyone. Ivan was just twenty-two. They'd met at the Renaissance Fair in Peace Park. Ivan was wearing a jerkin and tights and a hip pouch on a thin cord belt. No shoes. He'd gotten the outfit from his ex-girlfriend, Liz, who worked as a costumer part-time for the Little Coral Players theater downtown. The suede booties that might have completed his outfit were probably too small for Ivan's feet. It had started to rain, one of those sudden September squalls. Rick had said, "Your outfit's ruined!" and Ivan: "Oh, Liz knows me. I can't surprise Liz anymore. It'll be okay. Anyway, the show has closed up."

That pouty Slavic whine, snarling the sinuses.

In his country, Ivan had said, what counted most to smooth over a problem or situation was knowing someone. The director, the mayor, the police chief. Everything forgivable.

No one ever got mad at Ivan, Rick bet.

The two-week run of *Kiss Me, Kate* had ended.

And Ivan and Rick were about the same compact size and had undressed together.

"I can give you some jeans and a T-shirt and a sweatshirt. Stay as long as you like."

To call a place *home*, when the one who'd made it with you was not likely to return.

To begin to enjoy a little evening's life a few nights a week. Taking some ownership.

Ivan would vault through the high, narrow bathroom window, launching from a stump.

Rick's friend Joy had said, drinking a margarita, "What in the hell are you waiting for?"

"Oh well, a little heartbreak," Joy would say—capable of saying whatever was necessary.

GENE WAS QUIET today. Something was happening, a corner turned, a corner leading to a darker passageway. His roommate, Brian, had to be restrained, his movements so jerky and at times too violent for such a small staff—and Brian would weep about his mother in Little Rock, which led to frenzies of chin-jerks and bright, frightening stares and simmering denunciations, "You bitch!"

Or he'd mutter a soliloquy: "It wasn't the heat, man. I come from Arkansas, man. Try to tell me about heat? No, man. I know heat. I know heat I know heat I know heat."

"I do wish he'd shut up," said Gene suddenly but quietly. "Honey."

Confidently, smugly, Gene said, "He can't hear me. He's in Afghanistan or wherever."

Gene wouldn't eat. The tray was returned with its cellophane wrappings tightly intact.

And no TV. Gene had stopped asking and Rick had stopped offering.

The room was dim, so that you could concentrate on the clinical odors, bleach, armpit.

Brian calmed down, his medication taking effect, and Gene withdrew, turning away from Rick, and didn't answer Rick's questions, or snorted lightly at one of Rick's dumb observations.

"You're glad you're in the air-conditioning," said Rick. "It's ridiculously hot today."

Snort.

Rick was lying, which may be what it was coming to. To save another's feelings or keep a soul intact, a decorum so that the mask would not crack and issue tears and howls.

Neither had religion. Rick was insulting Gene. They were supposed to be honest always.

Outside the light died earlier each day—soon the winter solstice. Christmas was coming.

It came to him in the dim hush. It occurred to him that he was alone. Didn't need to be.

Only Gene needed to be, or had to be.

Foolishly a title for what he was working on came to him: *Life of the Iguana People.*

Then he thought, laughing innerly, *Now that's the limit, that's really the limit.*

Something his own mother would say. He got up to go, but it was painful, a rending.

On the other side of the vinyl accordion divider, Brian said, "Just listen to me."

He ducked over to Brian's side: "I'm listening, Brian."

He was handsome, his life would soon be over, his mind

heading out much sooner. He had been a lover to another man. It was hard not to fantasize about this, not the brutal and raw soldiering part but the tenderness, the most private and secret tenderness in love ever, probably.

Nothing.

"I'm listening."

Neither roommate said anything. It would be a good time to believe in heaven, even if it was only a temporary holding space, a way station between life's last flutters and black sleep.

RICK WORKED MORE. No one was making him, but he had a few requests for contributions, which kept him smiling when he was alone. Ivan's hours increased since the holidays were merry with backbreaking work. Rick took an envelope he labeled IVAN and put Gene's key in it and left it in front of Gene's favorite appliance in the kitchen, the Cuisinart food processor, which was now Ivan's favorite kitchen appliance. It wasn't meant to be a grand gesture, it was more of a humble Sunday morning offering of gratitude and praise along the lines of: *Thank you, Jesus, for helping me ace algebra this semester*. Or was it already too little, too late?

Before London, before they'd met, Gene was spending a lot of time in France. His Gallic mindset had stayed with him—and sometimes Gene would refer to Rick's *goût*, his *goût de vivre*.

"Sweetie, you seem kind of puny lately," he said. "I hope you're not losing your *goût*."

It might be a hungover morning after a late night at the bars, which here closed at four.

He'd quit those bars a while ago, needing to make sure Gene was safe at home.

He'd gotten some of his *goût* back at those same bars, but he was getting older, aging out. He relied on serendipity. He hadn't prayed on it or anything, but he'd somehow had faith, maybe because at this point he only stuck it in others. This had required training over time, once the sex between him and Gene had stopped. The other thing about Ivan's generation, besides the short supply among them of accountability, was their open-mindedness. Were they less materialistic? And this seemed to extend all the way back to their bodies. Rick was jerking off late at night when Ivan couldn't come over. He'd actually come to believe he deserved Ivan and Ivan's body, his butthole, which never seemed to loosen, Ivan who was less than half Rick's age. A top never got infected, or else it was nearly statistically impossible if not absolutely so. After Rick got the wet tights and jerkin off the boy (he remembered the light ass smell that would deepen in a bit), Ivan nudged him onto his back. Wildly enough, Rick's wang was sticking straight up. Ivan spit on it and rubbed saliva into himself and swung a leg over and straddled Rick and fucked himself down on the nice fit. And never brought up the issue of a condom. Ever. He was assuming something, God knew what, but a member of Rick's age group would not have frozen or hesitated but would have addressed the safety issue. Laid out the case boringly, established rules, clinically lectured on it as Rick knew he should, although he was lonely. And the warm damp-satin feel of his dick in the boy's asshole—no stiff dick knew a conscience. Rick's generation was all cads, but Rick was idealizing the kid because he was beautiful. He shuffled through all these tableaux, the ones of their weeks together, with their captions, *You didn't ask. You should've asked. You know others would've asked and what's wrong with you . . . Asshole like a pussy. A man-boy unembarrassed.*

Ivan was a gift from the gods. But he would leave soon, Rick could just feel it.

You could be a cad because at least you had a rubber. There emotional culpability ended.

He came and realized he had these feelings, coagulant and clean-smelling. Disposable?

"I don't think you trust me," Ivan said the next time. "You don't think I'm true."

"Of course I do. I gave you the key."

"It's not the same thing."

"I'm old."

"But you don't seem old."

"I'm really grateful."

"You don't act grateful."

"I have a lot on my mind."

"I understand."

Ivan lived in a sordid room blown about with clothes and tossed cigarette packs. Maybe he had debts. He mentioned owing his roommates two thousand dollars, which Rick gave him.

"There's nothing attached."

"There's always something attached."

These European youths, so realistic, so free. He wanted to grab some of that, fuck into it.

Ivan was living off the grid. He'd come like so many of the other Eastern Europeans on a visa for students and he couldn't leave for fear of not being let back in, and he said, "I want to go home and see my family. It's been three years, my father's sick, he smoked and drank too much, and my mother's sad and says she's afraid she will never see me again."

"We can get married."

Ivan looked stricken. He waited. Then slowly he looked expectant, quizzed.

Rick followed up, "After whatever happens, though, if you can wait just a little. This is a terrible time. I'd do it out of love, not obligation, you don't have to feel obligated. *Obligated*—"

"I know what it means, obligated."

"Then you could go home, do anything you want. We don't own each other, okay?"

"I know what marriage is. Marriage is serious. I would take us seriously."

GENE'S CELL PHONE was stolen. It meant almost nothing, of course. He'd been trapped in Nam and Greenville mostly, and in their earliest shared moments in London and New York, and he didn't seem to know he was in the Keys. It was only because a tech using the phone for Gene's speech therapy—having Gene speak to Siri, asking her questions—had come in and found it missing.

Rick got a call from the Monroe County Sheriff's Office, a Sergeant Luisa Gonzalez. It was nearly midnight, and her shift must have been about to end, or begin. "Mr. Sullivan, I just wanted to know if you have any receipts that the hospice care center can use for reimbursement. I know this might sound tacky, but technically theft is a crime. Hate to be the one."

"You're working late!"

He felt jolly because even though it was Christmas Eve he was expecting Ivan, who was working another late shift at a tourist seafood restaurant with a lot of needy, whiny diners.

"Well, sir. It's my job."

She wasn't picking up on the mirth. She spoke evenly, and already Rick felt inexplicably bereft, out-of-body.

He said, "I wouldn't know where to find the receipts. Let's just not worry about it."

"I understand you completely. Being that what has happened, I completely understand."

He stopped.

"What's happened."

"Mr. Sullivan, legally I'm not at leisure to say anything. You should contact the hospice."

He called the hospice, but it was Christmas Eve and the caseworker and the head nurse were both off for the holiday and he stared, stalking, collecting himself, but collecting himself why?

He got on his bike. They hadn't had a car in years. It just hadn't seemed necessary. He could do all his shopping and necessary errands on his bike: *A car, a car, my kingdom for a car!*

He texted Ivan. He'd be late. Something had happened. He'd explain later. What was there to explain? What had happened? His heart wouldn't quit doing the rumba.

They wouldn't let him into Gene's room. Already his bed had been cleared, cleaned.

They took Rick into an office. It was all very sudden. A heart attack. A mercy, actually.

They gave him a large Ziploc-type bag—thick, clear plastic revealing the last of Gene's effects, neatly folded T-shirts, a pair of sweatpants for his physical therapy, which had been worthless.

The bureaucratic mess of modernity. Accountability.

And he'd questioned Ivan's sense of accountability. Ivan

had only ever tried to get inside and talk to him. That's what Rick had needed: talking-to, feeding, lovemaking. Ivan was *noble*, possessing this poetic, almost medieval nobility, this modernized gallantry, a warmth of yore.

But that was the mood Gene's death had rapidly thrown Rick into.

There was a lookout they'd loved before Gene had become immobile. It was in the small, cliff-encased gorge of a town called Les Baux-de-Provence near the farmhouse they'd rented every August—a place for them to write lines and sometimes read them aloud over supper with friends or after the morning coffee and pastry. Their lives together were couplets, a good line being just everything.

They sat up in a café overlooking the valley. Gene drank lemonade—he had not touched alcohol in two decades— and Rick had two glasses of the local rosé because he was driving. The cliffs were pocked with caves where troglodytes had lived and, later, renegades fleeing from whatever kings.

It was the last high place before a plain, which, by turning left, you could inspect in all its flatness smoothing down to the Mediterranean. All the way, if you could just squint and peer, to the once-Roman town of Arles, with its ancient amphitheater and its more civilized tourists.

Civilized was a word Gene had always cherished, his head full of the American South, its inequities gradually being erased in the tears-moist clouds of nostalgia and primal yearning.

There, the end of a steep, raw, caching darkness,
and there, the beginning of human-wrought,
*   calmed-wave beauty.*

He was breathing heavily on the ride home. With maturity he should let his lines expand, be less terse, open up. He cycled harder, feeling his calves alternate their work with his thighs, a cooperating rhythm.

The Leisure Classless

HOMOSEXUAL LEISURE COMPOUND (palms, chlorine). Evening.

Outdoor hot tub.

They were telling me about a straight couple they knew.

"She was a stage actress and he used to run a big pharmaceutical. But down here, we're the perfect neighbors. At Christmas he started this thing of giving us sex toys. She *loves* that."

"So we got a bunch of stuff from Leather Chest in one of their gift baskets, by delivery."

"Gift bow and everything."

I was thinking that if they asked, sure, why not. Tip right into that. Get off, go home.

Then I went ahead and offered. I was that horny. And this despite their age.

"Any time you want it, guys, I'll just hike it in the air."

They just sort of laughed and continued soaking and lightly splashing the bubbling surface and once while none of us was saying anything the (even) older one got out to reset the jets.

The loss of Carsten had unsprung me. Where once I'd had my own German unicorn from Munich, where they breed them especially (all that social democracy granting leisure hours, time off for young Mutti und Papa, fresh food, a passion for soccer), I just needed someone, one after another, back there giving me grief. I needed to be serviced back there. This is the PBS version.

I started to get out and thought I should say something to save face, if that was possible:

"So I'm going out to the bar and doing some work, finishing an article due yesterday."

Here at Fantasy House I can lean this way or that, into leisure or else into my living.

"Oh. Okay. You can do that, work at the bar, write with all that distraction?"

"Sure," I said, and made a little innuendo-joke, though I don't remember what.

Anyway, they weren't really asking, they were just being polite. They were happy as is.

American manners. I study those. I study them by going abroad, on the cheap. Not that they interest me—I just write about manners since we are, as Americans, fucking freaks. I write about them to let them go in my mind, to feel free of and above them. Caught and released.

I'm so obviously a writer, right?

A travel writer, but that's just an outgrowth of my lifestyle. More professionally, I'm an accomplished guest. Inherited a little, but had all these contacts, not all of them rich but a lot of them. And most of them aren't sexual, most of them are women, in fact. I buy a ticket to a tony destination where they live and they send for me at the airport, have me driven me to their digs.

They live in nice areas, so I can expense what I want to (dinner out the last evening) and rent a car and see the harbor, the nature preserves, go to restaurants, write it up. Internet content.

Sometimes their drivers take me around, show me the old kirk of Glen Shee, take me to an inn near Balmoral for a luncheon in front of the roaring hearth on the house.

Not exactly professional of me to accept, but who's going to care what my opinion of the shepherd's pie is as long as I say it's traditionally prepared and tasty?

Look at the times we're living in. No one cares or pays much attention.

A digital blink, a data shrug. Everything is click bait for selling something else; so am I.

I have been known to be dodgy. Pick up the customer receipt when my hostess takes the credit card receipt, then send in a pic to my accountant, lying that I prefer to pay cash. Not getting rich, I'm breaking even. I have no savings. I'm waiting to finish the guest travelogue that inevitably is coming out of this mass of sloppy, somewhat careless blogs. A title: *The Unaccomplished Guest* (because self-deprecation is important). Or else make it *The Leisured Classless*. My savings are spare. I own no property. And my work is like vacation.

But at the advice of my potential editor, I'm leaving out the sex.

Which, again, there's not a lot of.

Except when I'm down here in the balm. (For the sex, I have a thin, wan journal.)

I take a little off the top in my tax reporting and my expenses to give myself leisure when I want to take my time contributing to the blogs. I have maybe twenty conscious years left in me and I want to mess around, and I'm not on the apps. I'm on the scene. I like talking to the guys, live men. And Fantasy House, the compound, affords me this, and I can just afford Key West.

I live in a friend's room off the kitchen of his Craftsman.

The freelance writer's life, not that different from an existence of promiscuity.

It is nearly a perfect life and I should quit dreaming of having my own house. My friend and landlord, Teddy, nearly lost his during Irma, when suddenly she'd curved right. The fucker was put together with pegs and came from the Bahamas where it was first pegged together, then unpegged later, loaded onto a barge, then floated up the Gulf Stream. It has stood up to at least a hundred hurricane seasons. It inhales then it exhales. Teddy is seventy and he huddled in the center closet with his cat, Lily, while I was off in Utah, where there were all these fires distant from my cabin scorching across the ranges—one more apocalypse deferred. But it is coming, a reckoning that's partly environmental, the other part neoliberal, the climax of greedy, need-heavy humanity. It's coming, you ready? Because there's a journalist social media–market for that, too.

What are these sodden roots and rotting branches? When the noonday sun peeks into the spaces between the wet branches? It can't get in to evaporate the water that decomposes things here so quickly. Rainfall feeding humidity turning wood into crumbles like termite leavings.

No snow or ice, just the polar system slamming into the warm moist air. Huge rainfall.

I think I'm going to call it *The Unaccomplished Guest.* Sounds about right. It's funny.

THEN I'M IN Salisbury, taking a look at the cathedral. My editor has connected me with a lady novelist. I'm not denigrating her. Her novels are capable, romantic, with a faint sexual odor.

Her husband is an earl, some lord. His ancestral lands sprawl. We walk through a forest on his land full of gorgeous, promiscuous blooming bushes, rhododendrons originally from Asia. Cultivars, adaptations. They bloom outrageously, fuchsia, sky, eye-harsh violet. My host says, "What perfect tarts, but they've been in the family forever, a *fusillade* of Wiltshire impudence."

He pronounces *fusillade* very Frenchly.

Whenever I'm in the UK, I always have to look up a word or two. Once I went pheasant-shooting in Scotland, in the highlands, having come up from the Mull of Kintyre. The laird there referred to himself as a "wingshot."

Well, we hunted in my family, too. We just didn't have words like *wingshot*.

Later, perhaps needing cash for the manor's upkeep, the woman novelist stops publishing fiction and becomes a hypnotherapist. And disappears into Facebook with 253 followers.

Understand, I come from trash. For my relatives hunting was for squirrel, an oily, mealy quarry. Some quail. Deer but my father decided in middle age that he didn't like venison's taste.

Northeast Florida. Hunting cabin. Gray greasy squirrel floating amid gloppy dumplings.

Those of my blood remaining there do not miss me. I don't miss them.

Between the Bible and the big bosses of the unionless, leisureless, and classless "middle-class" rabble, all hugely in debt—a term that would describe me in destiny before my gay escape to college, thanks to a full-ride scholarship—our family bonds were gossamer to begin with.

I'm the only homosexual in the clan. For a time my liberal cousin was like my sister, and when my father was sick, she messaged me (because who spends time on the phone anymore?): "You should go see him. He's just so pitiful. And your momma could really use your support."

That "momma" so offensive and egregious to me, and on my phone I typed, "Just no."

"Your daddy, remember how quickly he accepted you when you came out to them."

I waited. She was the first to offer me support when I initially came out.

"You have no idea what you're talking about. That's the version you got, the legend."

"What do you mean."

"Men from our part of the country all have to be the stars of their own heroic sagas."

"Now he wasn't perfect, but he was a good man and you know it."

"Again. Please mind your own business."

I sort of lost her, too. Haven't heard from her since the day after the election. We'd commiserated, but then I think she got like a lot of people, wait-and-seeish, and just gave in.

I was forty before I was able to lay it out candidly for people getting on my nerves.

"Well," she said, "I just know what I've been told, and that's all I know, but I know it."

As for Southern women, that's another story. Their garrulous way of acting objective.

The women in my family, talkative, breathlessly self-assured social hurricanes. Tribal.

Heathrow. Text from Teddy: "Irma a teapot tempest here, no biggie, just some mold along your doorstep. Hurry home and help with branches if you don't mind."

I'm on a low-cost carrier, where I'm suddenly charged seventy-five pounds for carry-on.

Teddy and I met at Fantasy House. He's from Alabama, and it was mostly started with fun and jokes, but there's nothing like two Southern escapees. He and I will get into kimonos and do scenes out of *Flower Drum Song*. We order out. We drink vodka. Go separately to bed.

Like I said, there's precious little sex in this telling that's not past or not pure imagining.

But there were times. There were times in my twenties and thirties, with women even.

I LOVED ANOTHER greatly once: Marion, the environmentalist half a generation older than me.

We met at a pollution photo installation at Customs House. Marion was friends with the photographer. My jaw dropped as I listened to her mic'd speech: warmly, almost intimately, she spoke about plastics in the ocean;

the photos were gorgeous, in the way that cancer cells captured by electron microscope are like art: colorfully hideous, perfect killers that are invisible to us and smarter than us because they're just doing their job uncomplaining. Marion spoke unhysterically and that heightened the effect of dread and looming annihilation. I was instantly enraptured, and I enjoyed pleasing her, keeping her house neat while she wrote her magazine articles, learning to cook vegetarian, and being criticized quietly, in that same undamning tone, for getting it wrong.

Before she died, in the hospital in Miami, she said, "I hate having to say we fucked up."

She meant humanity. As her adoring helpmeet, I knew this implicitly.

"Uh-huh."

She loved only plants and animals and waited then added, "But I think we fucked up."

I kissed her tan, leathery hand. I was losing my life by losing her—such a decade, when I almost had it together, and meeting Marion was like standing in front of a statue inhabited by the great fertility goddess of this or that ancient kingdom. I recalled the afternoon drinks I poured.

I said, "I know, darling."

She wasn't gaga, just exhausted from the process of letting go, tissue by tissue.

The hospital floor was a tomb.

"The world . . ."

"I know," I pursued, "the world is lost. We've lost the world, we've done a good job."

She curled her lip. The tan was evacuating from her beautiful, sun-ruined face. (She'd birded all through the southeast, knowing plumage, sighting evolutionary livery.) She sneered. I hadn't done enough, the sneer was telling me. Or maybe she just hated dying. She'd loved life because she'd watched it slip away all around her. It was her profession to get it all done. She loved life.

She'd never married but had a grown son, a corporate lawyer whom she didn't resent. It didn't even occur to her to disapprove of her own son for helping cause global mayhem.

"I could've loved you more, argued less. I could've been better."

"No, you couldn't," she said evenly, and I watched her all through the night, so shrunken.

Then I dreamed that she said, "You haven't listened to me or understood me at all."

I'd fallen asleep between four or five in the morning when the nurse woke to tell me.

MY FATHER HAD lost some of his money. When he got cancer I flew to Lake City to be near him. Jim had a drainage tube curling away from his abdomen and dripping into a plastic bucket next to his bed. On the ugly linoleum floor. I observed how disgustingly peeling and upcurling the edges of the linoleum tiles looked. Now I was more disgusted by the sordid VA facility (a come-down for my father) than I was by him. And in that moment, briefly, I felt pity nearly like an old love.

In the bright next day my mother drove me to the bank to open and look into their safe-deposit boxes. Amazing assets. I was now the executor. I took home keys and codes. Then my father recovered. Once, I'd recognized their marriage as what a friend had identified as this great love coupling, meant to dispel the want and neglect of what I'd known growing up. They'd paid more attention to each other than either of them had to the rest of us. Primally, I was glad of his recovery, and that feeling had lasted for a while—ending around when the love and pity did, too.

I wanted to believe I had it in me to survive long and hard, too, just through heredity.

We were on the phone some months later and my father said: "Well, I'll never go through fucking chemo again. Fuck that. Know what I'll do when it comes back? Get out a shotgun and stick it in my mouth and pull the goddamn trigger."

He'd served in Vietnam and talked unapologetically like a soldier and taken us to church.

They'd had five more years, more love for each other and more reticence, and even—I'd say—more diffidence and probably disgust toward their offspring. Since we'd survive them. He got sick again, as he no doubt knew he would. They'd said it would move to the brain next; it did.

So after seven years, according to the police report, he'd

taken out the shotgun, loaded it, and found my mother while she slept and taken care of her first. Life can be surprisingly ugly.

Then you move on.

NEXT I'M IN Tuscany, on the fabulous estate of two unrepentantly fussy queens. Olive groves, vines. A vegetable garden and, for the more leisurely inclined guests, a swimming pool and gracious gardens. The house itself has been expanded. I won't swim, ashamed of my torso. They are so judgmental that nothing escapes them. All is taste, manners. They drive me into Lucca for their special pasta, which is simple (it's good), and when I have to write home about it I brag about the freshness of the peas, the velvety simplicity of the elephant-ear pasta. I've had too much wine, it is pointed out to me. They laugh as we walk atop the medieval city walls: "Wine is the sibling of a meal. Let's get you home, you souse. We have a painting to show you. You'll be amused . . ."

I know what they want. I'm not going to give it to them, this understood privilege.

They're American, one rich, the other pretentious. The pretentious one talks much more.

The painting was from the Bourbon era, the last good one, they said—the Risorgimento a bourgeois nationalist turn in the wrong direction. I was supposed to resemble a baron but didn't.

They were supposed to be getting me into bed, me a generation younger, but they didn't.

They came from Chicago and had begun buying into their taste. And there I said it.

WHEN I'M AT home, I'm in Teddy's room watching cable on a big flat-screen TV. And all I need are cable news and PBS. The South Florida PBS I love because it's soothing. Nothing's so soothing as basic cable in the evening, when night has gathered above the back garden you can smell with the windows open, the air carrying the green and colored odors from the wet leaves and flowers, and you know not much is happening anywhere else on your island. No, taste and sex—to me—are the greatest violence, assaulting you, questioning your motives and impugning your worth. It is a nice thing to be a sentient mammal with language, without a past necessarily, without a thing called taste, and with your libido and hunger for sex and the questions it drags in its wake behind you. If you don't feel like eating, you don't eat anything. Teddy upstairs is in bed by six or seven.

Sunday PBS is my favorite, for its symmetry and logic. The British procedural detective drama I watch stars an actress who had her day in the nineties but waned because the films she'd been chosen to play the lead in were so painful to watch they lost every foreign Oscar. Whatever he had directed, I implored my friends to go out and see by this English genius. I won't say they lost me those friends, but I'll say with certainty I went down in their estimation. I was the snob—but I'm no snob! I'm the opposite of a snob! I'm the original of me, myself. No pretensions. I hope you can spy that. I come forward and lay out the truth of my simplicity. I'm not much.

I like spying out the formula of the British crime drama starring the Celtic actress—who should have won that Best Actress back when and, since she never did, is consigned to BBC.

Here's the formula. Something terrible has occurred in the city in the north of Britain not far from the Scottish border. Every week something terrible if not outright heinous, unspeakable.

Her lieutenant is taller, handsome, blond, but he's just learning, watching her move, act.

She has her gestures, working the shrug, the frown, her voice a kind of detached whine.

The gestures and voice are couched in what I call her patented bemused declarative.

I think this is what I relate to, her bemused declarative tone, when she cross-examines.

"And then what happened, dear. You had to make it look like an accident, didn't you."

You can barely hear the question mark at the end of every weary, bemused declarative.

The guilty are either rich or portrayed by sexy young, let's say it, flowers of Britishhood.

"And in order to save the affair and cover it up, you had to drown the bairn in his bath."

Initially I had to look up *bairn,* the Scots for "child."

Overall the series makes great use of *bairn.*

I LIKE TO be in for the night by four or five, though one evening I was running late, having been at the homosexual leisure compound. I'd gotten into a lovely conversation with a youth who was acting enchanted. I never understand young people who take an interest: What do they need of us when now they have everything? He'd left home, he said, suddenly. Left Montgomery. Jay was living at Fantasy House, where this account begins. I was taking an indoor hot tub. Kids now, or some of them, come swinging in naked. On the walls above the Jacuzzi, there's a reproduction of a Matisse, naked men with their hands enchained, dancing or greeting the sun. They enjoin with Nature, whatever, painted in acrylic (acrylic, I assume: more moisture-resistant) on the sheetrock of the hot-tub room. It serves. I sound pretentious writing that, but it does inspire. Ignore it, and it doesn't matter. It's part of the atmosphere. Nudity, good. Sensuality, premium. It's all good.

I WAS RUNNING late. I locked up my bike and turned to pick up my groceries from Fausto's.

A shabby figure of a man came loping along, his clothes

storm-wrinkled and dried again. His hair hadn't been cut in a while. He hadn't shaved. He stopped, turned in the wintering gray.

"Oh, wait," he said, complete stranger, and pointed at me. "I've got a story for you."

I was drunk and the next few lines are a hallucination, a melding of two timeframes.

But back to the hot-tub scene, and then forward to back home later.

"HEY MAN, IT'S so nice and warm in here. I'm dating the owner. I'm free to be, man, I'm free to be myself. You're so interesting-looking. How old are you? You look full of experience."

"A generous way of putting it, full of experience."

"I know guys of your generation are still uptight because of AIDS. I think it's more fun not to give a shit. I'm on PrEP, you know what it means. I can fuck, be fucked, not a problem."

I said, quite prissily, and insincerely, "I think we're getting ahead of ourselves."

"No we're not. You like my moustache? I'm sort of self-conscious about it."

"I think it's handsome. It doesn't work for everybody, but for you—"

He smiled, pleased. Then nothing happened. Nothing

happened and then I left the compound, not unhappily, but contentedly weary and completely impotent.

"WEIRD THING JUST happened to me. A girl was crossing Truman and she looked at me and she just sort of giggled, waving. Then she turned and stepped right the fuck into the path of a truck."

"LOOKS GREAT," I said. "It goes well with the angles of your face. I'm not looking to hook up."

I'll never get it up with this kid—too vital, too young.

"Oh no, man. I wasn't trying to say that. I was just talking. Where you from? I'm Jay."

The two older gentlemen who had told me the sex-toy anecdote earlier got in with us.

Jay got busy talking to them, too, and I knew: he didn't care about age, or anything else.

He just wanted sex for hire. And I respected that. Blog-wise, I too was sex for hire.

Travel is sex for the upper-annuated, the timid, and maybe the broken and disappointed.

More and more I know my place, the me I'm approaching.

IN THE LAST couple of years I loved, in quick succession, two younger men totally wrong for me.

The first was too young, I'll admit. He came and found me, then each time, each episode, went screaming out of my life, crying abandonment, then crawled back until by some lack of will he wouldn't crawl back anymore, bless him. I learned about personality disorders that way.

The other was closer to my age but couldn't find in me what he needed. Unremarkably, unsurprisingly, he liked them younger and prettier than me. And also he needed to be supported financially. I got it. Look at me, living behind someone's else's kitchen. But happily. Without a couplehood, I was free. I didn't have to buy two dinners out a night. Or any, if I wasn't hungry.

I didn't feel poor. I didn't feel bound. Just morning-horny. The acceptable age where a man could still fuck me—my back to him—or eat me out was going gradually up. Loneliness, not an issue in those twenty minutes. Transcendent pleasure that like the wonder-thrill of a nice dream doesn't last. I'm cursing and ordering and begging. I'm asking for approval, reassurance.

The unwritten law of promiscuous sex is obliging, whether through pleasure or abuse.

"That is my cunt! That is my cunt! My cunt!"

"It sure is."

"You like it?"

"Sure, it's okay."

※ ※ ※

"I LEFT MY mom and stepdad back at Wicker Guesthouse. We almost lost everything with Irma up in Big Pine, but we found out today, good news! We can rebuild the trailer. With government funds and help. And I was just thinking, DJ, pay it forward! And so I had thirty dollars and I see all these people without hope or homes or help—and I start taking people to lunch at Subway."

"That's wonderful," I say, wanting to take my groceries in and listen to Laura Nyro.

"But here's the sting. I want to do it again tomorrow. My mom and stepdad have gone back up to Big Pine to look into things, and I'm with the dog, and I just need ten-twenty dollars."

"I'm sorry. I have to go."

NOW THAT I no longer drug, I sit with my feelings. I'm lucky in that I have a place to stay, some money to eat on, but I feel on the edge as well. I have it better than some. I don't have it as well as others. I've lost my youth. Once I was beautiful. The loss of it I take as a sharp, black strike.

I go into the night's utopia. It's all wine and vodka.

My back doorstep smells of bleach, for clobbering the category-three mold.

But the garden remains, the bromeliads, the outrageous blossoms of bougainvillea, exotic bushes that climb and entwine and do well anywhere that's warm and there's enough rain.

You move away from the bleach smell and you smell color and green and warmth.

When I was five my father's baby brother seduced me. My father was celebrating a first million, and Billy was tagging along. My parents were drunk on the beach of St. Thomas outside the hotel ground-level door. Billy was between things, not knowing what to do after high school, not ready to commit to college—hoping to avoid the draft. I was five and Billy was eighteen. I think about it more and more, although I'd like to let it go. Years of therapy helped a little. Not that I blame him. I haven't for a long time, anyway. Sometimes I do lie here and think about it.

Stella Maris, Star of the Sea

(to Giuseppe Gullo)

KAREN HAD DIED on the trip down from Ohio. The heart: something they had known about for a while. She'd even sing jokily about it during rare drunken moments: "Oh, I've got a hole in my heart, / and that's a mighty bad place to start!"

They were over the Gulf. They'd connected in Charlotte from Cleveland—with two hours to go before the Florida leg—and they'd enjoyed barbecue and beer, and there was always great felicity between them, even after fifty years, especially after fifty years.

Dale had smoked until forty and drunk, on and off— and still he checked out in his annual physicals, was only on statins, and popped a beta blocker for his blood pressure but was otherwise hale at seventy-five. The dick still worked. That was one more pill. Only three pills a day and a baby aspirin, and he could do forty-five minutes of cardio three times a week and barely got winded. And all of that sweat and later the muscle-burn in his legs felt good. Satisfying. Rewarding.

Karen had not been so lucky. The atrial septal defect had been discovered late and so her cardiologist had warned her of the risks of surgery. Otherwise, she'd always seemed healthy. They'd never had kids. A little partnership was what they'd had. Dale had been in sales for Graustark Systems and Karen had volunteered to teach reading. For five-plus decades the two had taken a snug, comfortable voyage together toward the horizon, a cozy procession of trips and luxuries, high-quality durable possessions, and a fat, remunerative portfolio.

They were over the Gulf and, unusually, she didn't have a book with her. Earlier, they'd looked up from their phones—Karen would tirelessly keep up with their nephews and nieces—then, seeing the boarding call for their flight on the overhead screen, they'd thrown down money (Dale preferred to use cash) and hurried out of the roped-in dining area, laughing at first as they sprinted through the terminal to the nearby gate. Then she laughed less, while still in the mode of giddiness she got into whenever they were headed to Key West.

They hadn't been too late to board but Dale noticed a hectic shift in her breathing. They were about to step into the Jetway when a concerned, fretting gate agent invited her to sit in the lounge and collect herself. Then, when Karen got up, there was a little glazy craziness in her eyes, a bit of confusion as Karen dug around in her pockets and purse for her boarding pass. An unsteadiness, a confusion, the uncertainty of it tore quickly at him, pity having always produced in Dale the deepest affection. And he'd watched with a perplexing sweetness.

It passed. The plane left on time. To avoid what the pilot called "some weather over the Atlantic," they were rerouted over the Gulf. Karen was seated next to a window in business class, and it was her last glimpse of the famously intermingled emerald and azure: her words: "That's what it is," she'd said, and he took her hand, and he was almost crying even though she was better already and for all he knew, and trusted, it was just an episode caused by his not watching the time. What a jerk. He'd nearly killed her; no, he was grateful for another chance to be with her on earth. And when he'd woken up from his nap, she was staring at the ceiling.

KAREN'S LATE-LIFE revival (*renaissance,* as their friend Lyle had called it) came shortly after her first stroke—when they'd discovered the hole in her heart. Neither she nor Dale fished. Karen had hated West Palm Beach, Sanibel Island, Captiva. She had nearly liked St. Augustine except that they didn't play golf or tennis. Recreationally, Karen only liked smart talk, about books and things. She had had worlds inside her, great silent continents. She was the smartest person Dale had ever met, but she'd been raised Christian Scientist and had always avoided doctors.

He'd loved her, respected her, and no one was dearer to him, though secretly he'd wished for a young man to rival if not take the place of her. Instead of being able to give her the great passion of her lifetime, he'd given her everything else. So they'd traveled. Eaten well. Massaged each other's feet. Talked together into the latest hours.

And Hilton Head had been doubly cold—socially and climate-wise—in January, and good-bye Cracker South. He wasn't a raving liberal, but really, these Trumpy-Heads.

Something about the Trumpers you saw getting off the cruise ships here and doing the Duval Street crawl reminded him, this year, of their deceased friend Lyle, the folksy B.S.

"When did I last dare to visit Sugar Top Ridge?" a typical Lyle Pickett Roche novel began.

Dale could hear Lyle's genteel, gasped drawl whenever he'd share new work, a precise verbal prance that kept Karen enraptured, urging her to the edge of her chair as he read from his manually typed pages. He held up one starchy 100 percent linen sheet at a time close to his face and you saw the pinholes of light where he'd hammered the punctuation keys.

They'd met Lyle at a cocktail party given by the first literary seminar Karen had attended in the middle of a very late-midlife crisis. She'd get up early in the condo time share and leave Dale in bed, bike downtown, and attend dozens of speeches and panels. In the evening, there were parties and buffets (the registration fees were steep), and they'd dress in country club casual and Dale would hang back and watch Karen approach the featured authors, and soon he'd see her from across a brick patio laughing, holding a wine glass up to her shoulder, rotating it lightly against her palm.

And yes, Karen had blossomed a little. Dale was full of admiration as he looked around the venue, the Eastern European cater waiters so hot. He would not phrase this the way Lyle might, even though they were both gay. Lyle would have called them delicious and delectable, scrumptious, and Lyle indeed had done so later when they were all sitting together in his pretty wood-frame house and it was just the three of them and Karen had come suddenly, infectiously alive, completely snockered as Lyle camped. That was the exact conversational style Karen had responded so happily to. Dale wondered if Karen would almost have preferred Dale vamp it up every once in a while. But during the days while Karen was out, Dale masturbated thinking of the Eastern Europeans and some of the out men he saw holding hands on Duval Street. Now some of the younger, sissier ones were suddenly gorgeous, and this was Dale's own renaissance.

He had thought of men and boys his whole life, but down here was suddenly able to imagine using the word *beauty* for a male, not just for a little boy wheeling about in the living room for his mother and her guests. He liked the ones just leaving their boyhoods. He liked looking at their mouths, the curved-up corners where the upper lip overlapped in delicate flap-like fashion, just so, just slightly protuberant, the lower lip. He liked a little femininity but not always. He liked all of this with broad shoulders, raw flared hips and a big prominent ass. And he was afraid of these boys and shy around them as a younger Karen had been around boys when he'd first met her, even though she was four years older than Dale. He liked the wide chest he would've had to lift weights to get. And yet now the timid narrow chests were cute. He thought he didn't like the ethnics so much, the darker ones, although in his mind Jewish and Eastern European were suitably exotic. He knew he was *still*, and always would be, from the fifties. Once, his most imaginable taboo had happened. That time, a slight, pretty blond had taken a hundred dollars for drink money and let him watch his dark Dominican boyfriend undress, fellate, lick the ass of, and fuck him, while Dale watched, and was mesmerized, and knew secrets about himself. Seven years ago.

Once Karen had told Lyle that in West Virginia her great-aunt had self-published several poetry books eons ago—and had had something of a following in that neck of the Appalachians: "My Aunt Poppy?" Karen would remind him. "From Wheeling?"

Aunt Poppy was single all her life. For a while all Dale had thought was: *that lesbian.*

He'd grown up a good deal since then. Now he hoped Aunt Poppy had been gay.

The maybe-lesbianism now seemed more interesting than Aunt Poppy's poetry thing.

But once with Dale, Lyle had treated this revelation about Aunt Poppy's literary identity as though it were the most astonishing fact of both their existences, precious cargo for Dale to freight carefully in his mind—foretelling great potential in Karen's own personal life trajectory. Karen had never mentioned to Dale any literary ambitions of her own, only her love of reading.

He knew of secrets no one else did, not even Lyle. Her dread of doctors, her fear that having kids would destroy/ kill her. (She'd maintained a slender, boyish figure, never adding more than a pound or two to it.) When they'd met she was a part-time student taking night classes at a girls' college, working as a secretary in the daytime. It had taken her a year into their dating to tell him she'd lied about her age originally. Dale was an OSU junior dating a shy twenty-five-year-old. To save money while still working, she'd brushed her teeth with baking soda. There was no reason to be delicate or sentimental about Karen—only adoring, singing chesty praise, if he could do this without breaking up now.

"We must be cautious, proceeding with all manner of wisdom, keen, gravely argus-eyed! We must not treat Karen as some mere housewife, and yet we must be wise!"

As far as Dale could tell, Lyle no longer got laid.

A very long time ago, Lyle's tendency toward hyper-ventilative melodrama had made him famous. He was that thing that could give you notoriety, "a *Sawth'n authah*."

For years Karen and Dale had exchanged birthday and holiday cards with Lyle.

"He'll outlive us both," Karen said, but Lyle had died in bed alone, a massive stroke.

Dale had hoped that he would die first, leaving Karen to enjoy Lyle's attentions.

It was a beautiful town, Key West, the last bastion, the place of the just-misfits.

He would have pushed on, but Karen would never have heard of it. Her love of the place had been passionate enough for them both, until he himself had been infected.

That was it, wasn't it? Karen all along, seducing Dale, in her way?

FOR THE LAST several years he'd gotten them into a sweet dilly of a house on Amelia, three quiet, safe blocks off the main drag of Duval, gingerbread trim, tight coat of bright white paint, bougainvillea of magenta and violet and snow climbing over the picket; palms and a massive, shady gumbo-limbo to guard their room from its southern exposure; eyebrow windows, wraparound porch, a nickle-dull tin roof, a fully modern kitchen so they could have breakfast quietly, and where they could make a simple fish dinner or else pour their drinks and take them to the veranda. Karen loved the word *veranda*, once announcing over a spiked punch, "*Veranda*, a Portuguese word coming only into usage during colonialism."

One year the literary seminar had done colonial literature—and she'd followed that word *veranda* from the East Indies to the Caribbean, from every satisfyingly crumbly, lusty port to the next in literature, stopping deliciously, and unguiltily, in some part of Asia that Dale knew absolutely nothing about in order to inhale, for example, all of Somerset Maugham: "A poofter, you know."

She'd pronounced *poofter* as they'd first heard it together in Edinburgh, a weird word. A cute one, suitably prissy. A word they'd end up sharing. And then she'd laughed, high on books. High on fantasy. High on possibilities. A sensation rejecting quotidian disappointments. She'd spill her excitements out across the veranda floorboards, upsetting her drink, laughing.

It was their second life, but it was Dale's new life, and he was grateful for himself, and he was grateful to her for taking them there and for having *seen* it and for projecting ahead for them.

Not a dumb partner but his greater self, the definition, practically, of better half.

※ ※ ※

HE WAS ALONE in the house now. He wandered its rooms. He brought home a few bottles of wine and a fifth of rum and a quart of vodka. Dale did a lot of musing, but only when he drank. He wandered the town but avoided their old lunch spots. Dale didn't want pity. Dale didn't think he could bear it; he was in that curious stage of grief where he wanted to believe Karen might come back from Duval Street or any of the shops where she bought fish or flowers, whatever place she had relied on to create their long final act together: a last staging he'd imagined himself exiting before Karen. Dale talked to Karen, getting intoxicated. He sat on the back veranda with a glass and his bottle and the ice bucket, where no one could stop and offer condolences to him, or ask about Karen, or ask him questions, or just be friendly—kindness being the most intolerable emotional reaction, coming from the locals or anybody else.

HE MADE THE mistake of not eating and, knowing all along where he'd go, set out at nine or ten in the evening, although it may have been earlier since he'd begun drinking hours ago. The sun was down. He'd set out down Simonton, past the guesthouses, and avoided Duval. Turned right on Fleming. Dale had read about Fantasy House. He'd passed it on his bike several times, wondering if it wouldn't swallow him whole in one long episode of pleasure and debauchery should he enter the first time. Of course, Dale didn't believe in souls or God, since almost no one did anymore—although curiously Lyle had believed in that hoo-ha. Lyle, who'd never told him about Fantasy House. Lyle, who had pretended to find promiscuity perplexing. A Southern queen *would*. Drama, drama. Lyle had lived for love and attention and had given a lot of both, loved lovingly, and taken Karen to his heart and made her feel good about herself. Too, Lyle was pure decorum, breeding, from early on proud of his Huguenot background in Savannah, in the magical and mythical, the famous Southern United States. Home of Storytelling, *Love of the Art of the Tale*, blah-blah-blah. Dale loved Karen, who'd loved Lyle, who'd once goosed Dale—cornering him in his pantry, all inexplicably seething queen, Lyle with his eyes narrowed, up-close-ugly.

"What do you have planned behind that fine and dear and elegant woman's back?"

"Karen's back? What do you mean, planned?"

"I know about your marriage. Karen and I have spoken at some length about it. Karen's confided quite extensively and yet utterly discreetly, I assure you, to a degree—"

"You're not making any—okay, and Lyle? That's fine. That doesn't bother me."

Soon Dale would realize how often, all throughout his life, he would question the meaning or motives of the person talking to him: *What was that?* People baffled him, as though they were trying to, as though they were being thick on purpose, just for private giggles.

"So it's no secret. Big deal, you. Do you think I'm a chump? Do you think the world is full of chumps? Well it is, but I'm not one of them. I'm not one of those chumps. Do you get me, fella? Or maybe I am one, but I'm one of the smarter chumps."

He teetered slightly saying that last *chump.*

Dale had wished Lyle would stop saying *chump*—too goofy a word for an author.

Plus, he'd twisted it, the way he'd twisted his scenes and dramatic situations just to suit the melodrama of all that language. Lyle had tried to set the world on fire with his language, but the problem with language was how it got away from meaning and flew into space and destroyed itself. In thrusting, it burned too hard and incinerated, becoming an impactless cloud of gas.

"I need you to hear me." Lyle simmered.

"All-righty, Lyle. I'm all ears."

"That woman out there, sitting with those nice, decent folks? She is by far the finer and more valuable integer in this equation you have the tenacity and I'd say even temerity to call a marriage, that sacrosanct, most venerable and holiest of institutions!"

"I agree."

"Oh, you agree now, do you?"

"I just said that I do."

"I'm so sure. Oh, the mendacity. The arrogance," said Lyle, who stood almost three feet apart from Dale, and released humid gusts of repugnant sour-mash breath.

Dale waited, his nostrils twitching. Then he said calmly, "I've always been grateful for what Karen and I have enjoyed together, and she knows, dear."

"Enjoyed. Enjoyed. And do you suppose that in her position, as integer in this equation of absurdest calculation—which you have the arrogance to call a marriage—"

"Stop it, Lyle. Stop it now. You're starting to make zero sense."

He hadn't shouted. Neither of them was shouting.

"I'll stop it. I'll stop it—"

Lyle was half a foot shorter than Dale, but in his intoxicated state was bolder than Dale might have expected, quicker, launching himself on tiptoes and kissing Dale's lips.

"Would you still prefer that I stop it?"

"I would, actually, prefer that you stop. Jesus."

Dale wasn't mad. Now, as he chugged down the sidewalk along Fleming, he even recalled he'd been quite the gentleman with Lyle, but still forceful, peeling Lyle off of him, Dale's hands pressed on Lyle's bony, untoned shoulders: "Listen to me, sweetheart."

"Yeah?" said Lyle, wheezing, simpering a little. "Say it!"

"I'm not going to tell her this happened. But if it happens again, Lyle, I will."

"You're not going to tell her *what* happened?"

"Do it again, Lyle, and you're finished for us. Do you have that?"

And Lyle kept his distance from there on out. At first Dale had worried that Lyle would take the scene perversely as a sign of encouragement to keep going. The problem with prigs and prudes, they never took no for an answer. They lived without the freedom that said they could move on. Puritanism drove them ever back into the closet, looking to snatch that one conspirator in with them. They didn't understand, they were so desperate. There would be another lover, a fresh opportunity, inside their romantic heads. Inside they were perpetual teenagers.

HE SAT AT the bar, his back to the pool. He was going slow on his first tequila and soda, extra limes. This is what you did. Bought a day pass and they gave you a key to your locker. You got in there and took your clothes off, nice feeling. Hot shower. Stepped into the Jacuzzi, all hot bubbles and jets rattling your nuts around and hammering at your back with ball-peen precision. He'd just learned the rote, anyway. This is what you did. This was the way you did it to make it all feel nice, to make it work, to set you up.

Another guy comes in and seethes down awkwardly and jimble-jointed next to you in the Jacuzzi, your age or something. Nods. Kind of bashful high school locker-room stuff.

"That sure feels good," says the guy.

"Dudn't it."

A tad awkward, on purpose. A tad distrustful.

Pressed to it, he'd end up saying, "Thanks, I'm into younger men."

Nothing personal. *You don't need to go all what-a-cliché and that's-so-stereotypical and have-you-ever-tried-thinking-outside-the-box and do-you-have-any-idea-what-you're-missing?*

That might do it. He wasn't Randolph Scott, but he wasn't a lizard with a goiter either. He considered his body, his looks. He'd lucked out genetically, but also had taken precautions.

He'd always gotten his sleep. Watched his eating. Not drunk too much.

Then you got restless so you skipped the steam room and the sauna right there in the wet area and got the nerve up and stepped out of the hot, farty bubbles. You wrapped the generous striped towel around your waist and went out past the front desk into the tropical pool area. This place was a fucking motel from outer space; it was Nat King Cole meets James Dean. Shrimp cocktail and Manhattans on the side of Route 66. It was cocks and hard, flat, square tits, the chest having been the kicker from the start back in Marion, his place of origin. (Warren G. Harding, too. Maybe that town was all aliens, too.) Focused on the bartenders and, fuck, were they cute, but they weren't for you because that guy your age came out and saw the moon in your eyes and said, "You know all the boys from Eastern Europe, they're not gay, right? They're eye candy, but they are not to touch or suck or fuck or get fucked by. Not homos. That's how the owners like it. They don't want their staff messing around with the guests, which is only practical. It just keeps the whole membrane solid . . ."

"Okay. How's that work? And my name is Dale."

"Hi, Dale. You ask me what's the advantage of separating staff from patron? I'm an old-school marketer."

"So am I."

"Oh then, well. So you're familiar with the phrase goodwill."

"Nearly died on that sword," Dale said, "but I'm interrupting."

Jeez, that obscene hand! Was his own hand like that? Bones and jelly at room temperature.

"Any bad blood between staff and client, that's bad for management."

Dale nodded, heading into it with a cute grin: "But this ain't your regular, orthodox-type business setup. I mean, Jesus. Guys swanking around in the nude . . ."

The other guy said, "Hell, beating off in the lounge chairs right next to the pool. Every other corner you turn, there's an orgy in a guestroom with the curtains wide open. Hot guys, too, some of them. I hear the owners don't care for the piss parties in the gang shower so much.

Every once in a while you get a floater in the hot tub. How many times you gotta tell the guys to douche. You a top, too?"

"Okay, that's about as open and graphic as I need it."

Weird feature of gay life: never knowing if the other guy was toting up judgments.

"I get excited. I'm Ken Worth. Living in Mobile currently."

"Thought I heard an accent."

"If you did, it's through osmosis. Only reason I may've picked up this one's from selling chemicals."

"You mean you're not from Alabama originally."

"Indiana. But I got out of there. Got my divorce, got my kids through school . . ."

"Alabama's an improvement after Indiana? I'm from Ohio."

"My wife was a goddamn alligator. And the weather sucked. I like cute Southern boys, the ones that went to their moron dads' frats. Kappa Sig and ATO. Hot sexy dopes."

"Heh heh, I guess I kind of do, too. Boy-next-doors. Not all geniuses, but who am I?"

"They make 'em in the South more charming and hotter than anywhere else. Just pretties, charmers, every god-damn one. And they know how to keep it pure. At heart good Christians and good, clean, peachy-white boys. They got the best of everything, and they know it. Smilers. I don't denigrate them or their faith, I just don't share it. Though yeah, I have my doubts."

"Really nice meeting you, Ken. I'm gonna head out of here."

And he finished that drink and got up off the stool.

Racists. What the fuck had happened to the Midwest?

He wasn't entirely innocent himself, grew up saying the N-word, too, but Jesus.

"You don't want to go back to one of our rooms and catch a Netflix?"

"I really appreciate it. How long you staying, Ken?"

"Whole week. Just arrived today."

Dale said, "Oh goody, nice little stay," but he thought, *Oh shit.*

He needed some strategy if he was going to get through sticky situations like this. He wasn't just going to hike up his skirts and take off every time some guy got on his nerves.

That's what Karen had done, allowed him his feelings. Sometimes protected, sometimes encouraged him. He never knew what she'd say, but he always knew she'd have something to say, interesting, encouraging. He knew it just felt better to come home and tell her things, not every single goddamn thing, but it was fun to run things by her. And she knew it turned him on just being listened to. And he'd enjoyed getting her off, fingering her. It was the middle of the night, she scooted over, scooped herself into him. He reached around (they were both naked), and began to touch and tease her clitoris. He went in as she got wetter. He got her off, her pubic bone pressing the heel of his hand.

He was alone, without a partner to process this with, his buddy, co-conspirator. Was he just going to avoid this place for the next six days? Because he would. He'd even threaten it like that if Junior, what he called Karen in punk times, had been around to bounce things off. He never would have had his first intercourse with a boy, that is practically a boy, without Junior's bucking him up: "You're never going to know for sure if you don't go for it, darling."

He'd destroyed his mother's arrogant image with Karen's love. He'd done it on purpose. He'd fucked the guy, no Monty Clift, trying to push her out of his head, Miss Sunday School.

Junior let him bleed. Just say a cross or hurt thing to his mother and he got an earful of Presbyterian sarcasm like steel wool on scouring powder on marble. Once he thought the witch was the reason he was queer. Junior got that sorted out. He thought he could hide behind it and shrink from his sexuality. Junior knew how to use the technical terms without sounding creepy.

"I think your mother," she said, holding one of her two or three cigarettes a night, "made it worse, but God or whatever made you that way after the trip you made from your father's body to your mother's."

He thought of his childhood self as a fetus, slowly rotting while also gradually growing.

He only grew in Karen's light.

Karen's "God" was clinical, harmless, at the mercy of clean logic and DNA.

She needed to tell herself these things, talk an admixture of psychology and sin or moral accountability at least. She wasn't purely a saint. Rehearsing realism, was Junior. And he hid. How many guys hid behind the nurturing blind of their wife's skirt? She wanted to be the soul of reason for him, but the perfectly practical institution of medicine had frightened her.

And other women were especially good at making excuses for their men. Not Karen. She'd wanted him to face it, but maybe this had kept her from facing some of her own stuff.

"You're a good-looking man still, darling. Go get 'em."

He'd never liked his own looks, and his mother had known it. She'd spotted this early on, Miss Sunday School.

"Oh, you got all gussied up. Well, you're clean, I'll give you that. Now. Is the world supposed to throw you a ticker-tape parade? Is the world about to—you missed a few spots on those teeth."

Where was the kindness?

He'd been yanked from hell at Ohio State meeting Karen. Right away he'd gone crying into her arms, and had almost not respected her for letting him. Thank God he'd wised up. She got him wised up. He began to get defensive and said, "I can't believe you're letting me not be a man. What kind of girl looks at a wimp like me and has any respect for him, or self-respect?"

"Where did you get your definition of a man?"

They were all just starting to talk like that in the sixties, the decade of unabashed boners.

HE CRIED IN the house. He lay in bed almost till the light broke and drank no more and talked to his women, all gone, all gone. His first sweetheart. And the sour-ass Presbo matron of Marion, Ohio. He cursed her. He cooed at a ghost of Karen. He said, "Oh, Junior. I just wanted cock, I really just wanted some ass."

Their niece Janice called: "How are you faring, Uncle Dale? Should I fly down?"

"Oh, no no no, don't do that."

"Really? I'm just worried you'll get lonely."

"Oh, don't—just don't worry about that."

"You never were more than two days apart from her," said Janice. "You cooking?"

"Better than that, I eat. I'm rich. Key West is loaded with places to eat, good seafood."

"Oh, but that's not the same thing, Uncle Dale. Do you have all your old friends?"

"I'll make new ones. Some down here have died, of course. Happens. Karen and I would've been pretty much alone this year, anyway. It's pretty much a clean slate now."

"What happened to that famous writer friend of yours, that gay famous writer?"

"Oh, he's been gone a lot of years now."

"Aunt Karen kept him alive."

He considered this. Yes, in a sense, it was arguable.

"She had an altar to his books. Kind of a funny character. Nice. Treated Karen well."

"Oh, I remember. When are you coming home to Ohio?"

"Not anytime soon," he said. "Our share is up in a few days and I'm going to find a new place. Economy's not doing so hot so there's kind of a glut—I might even have the pick of the rental litter. Don't worry. But I miss you, honey."

"Oh."

There was a wistfulness in her voice as she sensed correctly that he wanted to hang up.

"Aunt Karen was really proud of you, Janice. How's the brood? How's Mitch?"

"We're all fine. There's just Juliet left here, and it's her senior year in high school."

"That's shocking! You and Mitch must be pretty, what, knocked out by that?"

"I don't know what we're going to do alone together.

It'll be like learning all over how to be married. You and Aunt Karen must have experienced that pretty often all that time together."

"You mean because we didn't have kids, and needed to come up with conversation?"

"Well . . ."

"We never got out of the habit of conversation. We were two peas in a pod."

"Oh . . ."

There was a weep in her voice, but a hopeful one. She wanted to keep talking.

He didn't.

JANICE HAD GOTTEN her education and taught elementary for a while, but her husband, Mitch, who had a furnace and fuel-oil business, wanted her at home taking care of all those little Catholics.

Columbus was calm but dreary. Lots of furnaces, fuel-oil tanks, college kids. Lawyers.

Lawyers burned everything to the ground. Dale had gotten singed a few times in his line.

Worse, he'd watched a nephew get fleeced, flayed, and torched on a settlement bonfire.

Christ, was he really going nuts now because he and Karen had stuck it out together?

He called the rental agency and told them he was leaving earlier and the woman was shocked. No one ever wanted to leave early! At the airport, people cried into their fruity frozen drinks and sank back into reality.

"It's all fine. It's not like we're dying to go. Just wanted to let you know. That's all."

"That's good of you. Since it's a share, we don't really have anyone needing in early," she said. "I can give you your deposit back after the inspection, but I can't prorate your time."

"I don't mind. Just a change of plans, unfortunately. I hate to scoot out before I have to."

"Oh, don't y'all just? Have you guys made it to the butterfly museum yet?"

"Actually, we never have. Next year, maybe. Time just gets out from under you."

"Ain't that the sucky truth!"

He could almost date her by her idioms. In her forties or fifties, what used to be a kid. Just ten years or so older than their niece Janice. He needed to stop thinking "we."

"Anyhow, I don't relish it."

"Can I ask, did something happen? Is everything all right in the property, or with you?"

"We've got a big family back up north. Never know when they'll need you."

"That's a proud thing to be saddled with," she said. "I couldn't have said it better."

Fucking Southerners. They even wanted a capital *S* at the beginning of their moniker. But they had some of the nicest real estate. He was sick to death of the phrase real estate.

He wanted off the phone. Couldn't concentrate. Maybe Janice had been hoping for an excuse to get away from Mitch, a galumphing bigot and buckethead. And Juliet— teenagers liked acting independent. It was their proving ground in life. Karen had been the one to mend all ties, hold a sense of unity in the extended bunch together. She was just an aunt, but her voice had always been a calming, ambient influence. All Dale ever had to do was work and pay the bills. And act sweet. That wasn't so hard, being sweet.

THEY'D READ SOME Homer back in Marion at Harding High. Ned Grant, doughy former stud-guy, war veteran. When he read out from a book, leading the class, gradually asking the pupils one by one to take over for a stanza, his voice began to hum, snarl, and bellow. He made the consonants precise without being prissy and wet (the way Lyle would), the *a*'s and *o*'s and *u*'s all full—and he was a different person, then, for a fellow so timid just before (pushing his glasses up the bridge of his nose as the classroom was filling every morning). You could see the strong, pale youth on the battlefield a decade ago. You could just see the hurt but dignified seriousness from looking at him and his wife, Rosalyn, sitting in the same pew near the back of St. Andrew's on Sunday, practically hidden away whenever she could make it to church at all (*alcohol*, was the verdict), watch how he touched and put his arm around her while the congregation bowed—his Rosalyn still hanging on to her redhead good looks and creamy smooth skin. You could see him taking her when he returned from the war. A *Stars and Stripes* reporter at Anzio and D-Day, sent home before the Bulge, his grenade-shrapnel limp humiliating him—except whenever he moved from text to text, stepping a little this way or that, his leg pegged and gimp, gut sagging under an ill-fitting sweater, the worn knit stretched, puckering, his complexion a drained beige, as he read:

> *Then I was driven by foul winds for nine days on the sea,*
> *but on the tenth, on the tenth, we reached the land of*
> *the Lotus-eaters.*

This basso certainty Ned Grant put into it. He might have eaten the flowers, been blown off his course in a hospital ship and eaten the flowers that put him in a drugged contentment that kept him away from his Rosalyn until somehow a rescue had occurred. He'd been airlifted off that wonderful seductive island, never to know the spells of pleasure again. Or so Dale fancied. And once he'd said offhandedly to Dale after class, when Dale complained of having too much homework, "There's a writer, I forget who, that said a life of pure pleasure is melancholy."

Dale had waited near the desk, while Ned Grant pretended to remember who it was.

"Anyway, it was somebody really accomplished."

Sometimes Ned Grant's melancholy seemed put on, until you saw him with Rosalyn.

IT COULD HAVE been called The Lotus House, it was so dully, slowly, grippingly seductive.

Three-fifty a night and even though he was famously cheap, or conservative with money, he liked saying, this time he didn't give a shit. His expenses now had been more or less cut in half.

He'd always let the smell of his money do the fishing before the reeling in. He had paid for sex, usually. But he hadn't exactly confessed it to Karen.

She knew. Junior knew everything, not that everything had to be discussed.

And then there was the kind of paying that wouldn't have surprised her, buying the boy a few dinners, getting him drunk, taking him shopping later. She saw the monthly credit card statements. Long before he'd let his queer out, he'd gotten into the habit of letting her write the checks. She wouldn't mention the charges.

So how had he gotten here? They'd given him a room in a secluded corner near the ice machine and behind the maid's closet, where the nougat-hued Eastern Europeans came and went picking up and dropping off equipment and supplies. Where a window should be, there was an outdoor stairs going up to the second floor. The last thing available at high season, little natural light. There was a high-up narrow window—was it called a transom?—in the bathroom. The damn place was a clean, tidy warren. He'd UPS'd Karen's things home to Sandusky. And when he got home he was going to ask the girls if any of them wanted any of it. He would not go home soon, a thought that was icy and remote, terrible, stupid, not to be thought about if he could help it.

And dreams in the little clean, tidy warren after the margaritas and tequilas. Distant cities and far-off times, younger selves, a pretty, hippie-ish Karen, a more innocent, earnest life together. They'd seen enchanted Rome as lovers almost, an atmospheric joy.

His father had briefly gotten rich during and right after the war, until the big companies in the line of cleaning and "personal" hygienic supplies for public restrooms had cut the middleman out for good. Until his father was forced to drive around with his Buick's trunkful of supplies for public restrooms—with toilet paper and glass cleaner and toilet-scrubbing chemicals. Until the old man had been reduced to a fraction of his previous worth and wealth and died suddenly of a heart attack at seventy, leaving only twenty-thousand dollars to Dale's stepmother. Dale had expected zilch—and got it. Dale's sister was impoverished. Dale was expected in his success to cover the rest of his family. He liked work. He hated poverty. Success for Dale left Christ out of the sum. Dale had been named for that half-shyster, half-decent guy Dale Carnegie. Carnegie had maybe never mentioned pleasure. Maybe pleasure was a sin for Carnegie, a curse word.

He lay in a towel. He left his door open, his imagination on the sexy Eastern Europeans.

They came and went, he reached under the towel, snagging and tugging.

He got bored lying there, aware of his swelling stomach, attracting no one.

He got up and put on a pair of khaki shorts and a T-shirt. He made for the bar.

There were so many gentlemen. That was the conceit, the gentlemen of all ages.

A blond came up to him, saying, "What's your name?"

"Dale."

"Dale? Are you from the South?"

"I was named after a famous speaker. He talked like a preacher. I'm not religious."

"Whatever, like I care. I think you're really hot."

It was shooting fish in a barrel. He had money, all he had now was scads of cash.

The boy was perfect, a Quebecois from a small shitty churchgoing heathen village. He danced downtown at the venues, liked walking around talking to the guys on the deck by the pool, swinging his fat whopper dick. Every trace of his body was the same even olive. Back in the cramped room they kissed and the boy made all the moves, in a mechanical but hot rote until the rote included trying to sit on Dale's face. An odor of intermingled mildew and marinara.

The long and short of it was this. He could buy sex forever. He was buying sex left and right in these weeks. Buy them drinks, pick up on their innocence, their cheer, listen to their occasional sob stories, and what paralyzing, mind-numbing stories some of them were: stories of abuse, painful material want, shameful poverty, lack and need, youthful loneliness, and heartache.

They didn't act sentimental or nostalgic or put-upon. They were poignant, easy lays, they didn't ask for much, and to him money and cash and drinks and meals were nothing. For the first time in his life he was blowing wads of cash, the more, the better, the happier—exhilarating.

The boys made conversation unboring, cleared away the need for corny, porny innuendo.

Dale didn't cry now, though occasionally he felt like it. He slept good, hard sleeps, waking at four in the morning and lying there, alone but not always alone, and when not alone trying not to think about anything at all unless the boy next to him set his thinking in a different direction, reminding him somehow of Karen (he never spoke of Junior with these boys, not yet). His latest was Robert. Robert was the first to go quiet for hours, and that made it easier to keep him around when Dale thought he might get a headache, or just wanted to think blankly and not listen to some more blabber, with Karen hovering off a ways still.

The situation was this: Robert was black and his mother was Austrian. He could quote a lot of poetry, and he counted Nietzsche, whom Dale had only heard of, as a poet. Robert's father had been a soldier, so much romance in the backgrounds of some of these boys. Dale got caught up in their testimonies, but gratefully Robert's was delayed and would start up only after hours of sleep after sex and wakeful silence. The others' stories were almost old melodrama but involved opioids and firearms and crashed sports cars. But Dale could play with their genitals while they were talking, reach behind and finger the cleft, kiss a body part, bite a tit. But Robert's body he hesitated to touch until Robert lifted and pulled Dale's hand onto him. Robert was different, he was soothing. And the fact that he was smart and didn't worship money reassured Dale.

Eventually—after Dale had learned nearly everything else about him—Robert had said that he lived in the mangroves—and Dale asked what exactly the mangroves were. Condos?

"You know out near the airport right next to where the condos start? People live there, homeless. We are all homeless. We're the last pioneers. I didn't have to leave Chicago, but I left Chicago. I was so disgusted by the direction this culture was going in, is still going in. You can live very well out there. I have a tent. The mangrove people respect each other's property; it's not stereotypical. And do I seem stereotypical to you? But we're building a new life out there. We're starting a new thing that will redefine humanity. We're resisting AI. We're resisting the status quo. We're resisting a life of toxins and toxic relationships and the dehumanization of our souls, of our souls. This may sound like a reach to you. I don't want it to. I want to enlighten you. I want humanity happy. I might sound dreamy, but I don't mean to be. I want to be light and fun and hopeful. Hopefulness is, you know, what being human is about? I have a degree in sociology and the humanities and I've translated Kant and Nietzsche and my favorite, my really very favorite, Hesse. You like Hesse?"

"I've heard of him, but I can't say I know anything about him, Robert."

At first Robert had seemed so unextraordinary to Dale, probably just because he was black, but when he spoke, he shamed Dale—who now knew he understood next to nothing about the world, about America. Robert was middle-class but was black and educated, and this combination threw Dale. It shouldn't have, he'd worked with many black men and women at Graustark. But Dale had never thought about any people of any color. He was learning an attraction, yet he was so far behind so late in life. They were just there, looking on, as Robert looked on, waiting.

At one point Dale looked away, he was so embarrassed, almost full of shame, an unaccustomed shame, but he'd recovered. It wasn't his fault. He was old, too old almost to be the queer he was.

Robert invited him out to the mangroves to stay in a tent with him, to show him what real life was like, but it sounded uncomfortable, awkward, buggy. Robert didn't have the money to keep coming to Fantasy House every day. Dale gave him two hundred dollars extra after their final sex—which Robert said would see him through the next couple of weeks. Then Robert seemed to evaporate. Hundreds of dollars total, which made Dale feel cheap. Fantasy House had a rotating cast, which only made it more enticing, more like the Land of the Lotus-Eaters. Whenever he began to feel bad about himself or the last boy, a new one arrived, someone new, a shiny object. One day he didn't get out of bed because there were no shiny new objects, and he needed the rest. Which was a way of coming to a place where he could think about Karen less.

Then he got a message from Robert, who was now in New Orleans. Robert had abruptly moved. Could Dale wire a thousand dollars to his account? Dale didn't hesitate. Well, not for more than a minute. The message came in while he was absorbing another tequila. He asked Petr the bartender if he knew where he could wire money, and Petr said, through his nostrils, "Wisstern Union."

In the middle of this Dale was wondering if he'd been

duped by Robert, and was about to be duped by another thousand dollars. He didn't think so. He didn't care. He'd stopped caring.

Petr then found the link for the Duval Street location for Dale, and Dale got up. It wasn't easy. It was the middle of the afternoon, sunny and hot, and the shade was hard to leave. But he'd developed a little rolling thunder habit with tequila, a mariachi parade, if such a thing existed, that got louder as the drunk came into greater focus toward evening.

If he didn't do it now, he wouldn't do it till morning. Did he care about Robert? He loved Robert platonically, now that the sex was over. Yes. He was learning, he told himself, to be gay and good both. Really committedly gay and not a secretive or prejudiced person.

Was his heart committed? Was it capable? The much younger man was someone to notice, as he'd noticed him, pay attention to, respect. Maybe Dale was now less racist.

He wouldn't know for a while. But there were those he wanted to love.

And because of his age, his love would likely not be returned in the same way.

The woman behind the bulletproof glass was used to drunks shuffling in to pick up a rescue bundle or explain a situation, he felt. He was learning to be a drunk, too, an elective loser here and there, debauched and full of free will and free-wheeling and okay.

Miss Western Union thrilled him by not smiling until the end of the exchange.

His life proceeded at Fantasy House a while longer.

TOPHER WAS A young architect staying in a nearby guesthouse with his family. He was so small and teen-like it was difficult to imagine him being old enough to know what to do with his dick other than jack it off. Which aged Dale. These kids were fucking as long as they'd been playing video games. Topher didn't play video games. He seemed to have a contempt for a lot of things people his age or older or merely drifting through life did. But Topher had a thing for Dale. He never turned away but paid close attention. He said something affectionate looking at Dale, or said something, looking at Dale, perplexingly negative about his own generation of Americans. He maybe drank too much, or too fast, as he had when they first met by the pool.

He said, "The ancients would laugh at us. Look at us. We're so obviously about to get into bed, or maybe we aren't. They'd laugh at us about that, too. But mostly what they'd laugh about is how far we have not come, just by emulating the ancient world shabbily and by copying their mistakes—but that's as it should be! History is repeated patterns. All is contingency, everything's expected, if only we'd open the fucking books and read them, we'd learn."

Topher waited, and would wait for as long as he had to, Dale felt, for Dale's response.

"Dear, I feel like half the time I'm talking to you I should have a dictionary."

"Ha ha, I get that. My father made me learn a word a day. It's our *language*, Dale!"

Really Dale had no idea what Topher was saying. He would have thought he was crazy, but Topher seemed to know enough about the facts he threw out to make sense out of world currency problems or explain the benefits of Bitcoin that it temporarily put Dale and his worries about the immediate future (which at other moments Topher apocalyptically seemed to be canceling out as a possibility altogether) to rest. There was no true rest but in the young man's olivine or sand-green or faded birthstone eyes. Soon, Dale didn't have to talk. That was restful. He could watch the kid-man's eyes if Topher wouldn't shut up or draw a breath.

Half their time together consisted of confusion, punctuated by Dale's hard fucking.

He fell right into Dale's arms, and it was so inexplicable. Dale was sitting at the bar by the pool and this young man, a washed-out strawberry blond, was lounging and got Dale in his sights and was smiling. Topher was completely naked. He didn't bother to wrap a towel around himself. He didn't need to. He carried his almost-empty drink from his lounge chair over to Dale and said, "Wait,

I've seen you here. I'm staying in a guesthouse, but I have a day pass. You're distinguished. I'd say you're intriguing."

"You'd say that except for what?"

"I retract the notion of qualification."

"You're running on empty," Dale had said, and, "What is it you're having?"

"Gin and soda, no fruit."

"Put that on mine," Dale told Petr, "if you wouldn't mind."

"Thank you. I'm down from New York, on a budget. I have lots of friends here, but this time I just wanted to do it with my family. Have a change of rhythm so to speak. I just wanted to have a good time, you know, and be with my family? They've never been here. And I think family is so important, and don't you? I've recently broken up with my lover, Ricardo. I need an adventure, and needed to reconnect with family. Wait, do you have family? Looking at you, I'm betting you don't. Or you just have a daughter, grown."

"Which question am I answering? No kids. I recently lost my wife."

"Oh, I'm sorry, Dale," said Topher, and touched his elbow. "You seem loving."

Somehow this wasn't as patronizing to Dale as it might have been a year ago.

"We didn't fight a day in our lives, not for more than an hour, and then rarely."

"I'm not surprised. You seem to have that loving sense of mature peace in you."

"I don't know what it would have been like to have children with Karen. Karen was special, a little delicate. Sometimes strong. I think she could only be happy without children."

"I get that with some people. But right now I'm really close with my family."

"Did something happen between you guys? That you should reconnect?"

Something about his words told Dale that Topher wasn't completely out of the closet.

"Not especially," Topher said with a smile becoming a gulp. "It's an adventure."

"Oh. Well. Then let me be part of your adventure."

Dale hated it the instant it came out of him, like a rotten fart he couldn't reabsorb.

But Topher, in a way, wasn't apparently listening too closely. That was just a trick he pulled whenever he had something else on his mind, an idea, an ideology, something. He was caught up in his own internal narrative, whatever it was, yet he was really somehow into Dale.

"Oh, I love your shape. I love your gray! What do you do? Are you retired?"

When they were in bed, Topher didn't stop talking, pure energy. He was life alive. Every sense on turbo, and that motor mouth.

He said, "So all your people are from Ohio, mine are from South Carolina and the Outer Banks. My parents were developers, they were up until recently. My father had to file Chapter Eleven. It was the usual, the decline of civilization. That's what's happening in our culture, don't you agree? We've been—America's been—in a steady decline since, oh, after World War Two or at the very least the fifties? It's a moral failure as much as a sense of inertia. I mean . . ."

"You weren't even around after the war. I was a kid. There wasn't any decline to anyone I knew. I think you've got your sense of things mixed up, but you're cute and young. Smart."

"I'm forty, actually, and I've read a great deal on the subject, like about unions."

"Nothing wrong with unions. I hate it when people call them communist. There are extremes everywhere. The ones I don't like—oh, fuck it. Let's just skip it."

"Why? Don't you think this is fun? Isn't debating what we're supposed to do?"

"I never learned it. I never was in the debating club. I just don't like arguing."

"It's what democracy's supposed to be all about, or was supposed to be."

"I was just a kid, buddy, but I was there. It wasn't paradise. Nothing ever was."

Topher shrugged, sure of himself but also in need of

affirmation. Dale was ready to give him some by eating out the boy's asshole, in the cleft between two really nicely carved cheeks. Buttocks that Topher himself compared to those on the statue of the Roman youth in that statue museum in Rome behind the whatever, also known as the wedding cake, the lover of the emperor whoever. Who when the boy died took it out on all of Rome. On and on he went, about how everything was connected to everything else, which it certainly was not. Patterns, lessons. But Dale's appetite had begun keening to Topher, even as Topher said a world with cars and TVs was absolutely no different from ancient Rome. Dale could afford to go to Rome anytime and enjoy it for all the ways it wasn't like anything he knew or had known back here. You could walk and dream a story that never happened, just in that setting. Dale didn't care what Topher believed. He liked licking the auburn patch between the balls and hole.

He said, "Maybe it would be better if we just stopped disagreeing. Found a neutral topic. I'm starting to get the idea that I'm really more an audience for your ideas than a sex partner."

"That's not true. It's just, these things matter to me. To us. It's my future."

"Boy, you're telling me."

"Just let me say one more thing."

"All right, my young friend. Shoot."

"It was only natural, it was actually predicated on

the general Roman decline, that Constantine should Christianize the empire. And, thus, began the melding of histories, that cynical people call myth. It's syncretism, that's the whole game! The virgin, the son, the resurrection, running like blobs of fresh paint on a warm day, with classical gods. This only shows the inevitability of the repetitions and cycles of history all over the world. Waves."

"Okay," sighed Dale.

"But do you see where I'm coming from?"

Dale had never figured anything in history was inevitable. He'd lived through so many decades he could never have predicted, starting with Vietnam's escalation, that criminal Nixon. After Nixon, all bets were off—and he told Topher, "I don't agree with you."

"History is on a spin cycle, is all," said Topher. "It's the same issues owing to our human natures. We're entering a phase like in the late republic, or early empire. This is due to the total criminality and bad faith the deep state has absorbed, as all governments over time do. Ha ha, also known as corruption. Ha ha, also known as venal, sinful humanity. Aka moral rot."

"Sounds really Catholic."

"Ha ha. Well yes, perforce it does lean that way. I will tell you, I used to be a real atheist, but then I realized, what's the use of that? Not to believe in anything except what happens supposedly randomly, haphazardly? That's ridiculous, that's not being human. I do think," Topher continued in a tone combining loathing and delectation, "Catholicism's the next wave, it's time for it again. Or at least that's how it picked things up after the fall of the empire."

"History wasn't my strength," said Dale. "I always fell asleep. I liked literature."

"Perfect. Dale. Have you noticed that literature itself is in decline. No, wait, fuck that. Going back to my family, my parents were born right after World War Two and they had every reason to expect the best from this country."

"That sounds a lot like me."

"But you lost big-time."

"No, actually, I got lucky. I worked hard, but not that hard. I had a soul mate, my wife, Karen. And she gave me support. But I did thirty-three years with my company and things only got better and better for us, overall. There were hard times, but I survived."

"Okay, that's exactly what I'm talking about. You got lucky, not everyone did."

"I just said that."

"But the promise was otherwise."

"Yep, you're right there. It was a naive promise. And I got lucky. I got rich."

"My parents did not. They got into debt. But they were deceived, but maybe they were complicit in the deception of themselves. Maybe the deep state had a part in absorbing the country's resources. Maybe we've all been deceived. I persist in blaming Hillary, for one. And that cynical, criminal hoaxer husband of hers. But Hillary!"

"That nice lady? She seemed so sincere."

"She was among the most complicit. One of the warmakers, debt consolidators, usurers. I don't want to argue. I can see you're spoiling for a fight. Just to say, I'll inherit nothing."

The scenario Topher spun was not unfamiliar. It tugged at Dale's heart. It wasn't untrue, some of it. Dale thought of his heirs. They were going to get a lot. When he was dead, finally, he wouldn't have regrets or guilt. But Topher had been cheated. It was sad. But a deep state? It was silly to think of it as anything but a clock repaired too many times that finally runs down. It wasn't random, it wasn't unpredictable, but it hadn't been engineered or master-minded that way.

Topher's limbs were sheathed in milky skin, so soft you might cry. And Topher's parents had done everything right, as so many Americans had done things right, and debt was a national malaise. Dale and Karen had not had children to send through college. This was just a phase for Topher, Dale wanted to believe. The bitterness would get diluted by future contentments maybe.

"They're traveling around now. They filed for bank-ruptcy and that meant they couldn't take inheritance from all our older relatives. They were on a boat sailing the coasts, now they're in a camper driving around to national parks. This is the worst country for people of means with so much on the line and that bought all the lies. They worked hard. They trusted the state, they trusted the banks, and they thought all those were separate institutions, but they're all one—"

Dale said, "I never know what to do with that. The Deep State."

Topher looked at him long and laughed, saying, "You haven't studied it, or read about it?"

Dale said, "I just want to fuck you."

The kid had a degree from Princeton. He was smarter than most, maybe his smartest yet.

It took some fucking to quiet Topher down. In the middle of it, it was all sweet.

Every young potential lover had a screw loose, it seemed. The gay world, so romantic in its lostness, its need to assert itself. And why not? It had been repressed for so long.

The younger man's arms were strong. His ex-navy father had taught him calisthenics, he did them every day, Topher said. Not a word against his father or parents. And as for the president, Topher said that things were headed in the right direction, if only it weren't for the media. What was needed was interruption, chaos, the reignited and restoked forge of forces.

Already, Dale knew that soon, very soon, he was headed back to Ohio.

"Don't you agree?"

"I was never asked in all my life whether or not I agreed. Or I was, but it was implied that already I did, so it was easy to nod. You seem nice. You're unbelievably handsome. I'm just not interested in this subject. I just want to live out what's left and be relatively comfortable."

"Do you think you'll see Karen again? Do you think you'll rejoin her?"

"I really do not, sweetie. Again, I don't have any faith."

"We've been in steady decline, we've lost all faith. The proof is us here, right?"

"This is a bad thing?"

"It's not a bad thing, but don't you see, it's a symptom?"

Dale's days now were strange, a queer lullaby, stranger than he might have imagined. He missed Junior. Then it was as though she were advising him from the dead, not truly, but as he'd known her. Her practicality. In the world of boys, it seemed, you were always revisiting the past unsatisfactorily but sensually. Boys, after all, were descended from men, and being a man wasn't such a great thing. It didn't matter what you did in a gay world. You could make things up. You could bug out. No, to be a woman was the future.

The Other Way Out

(to Joy Williams)

WHAT DID SHE *think* would happen?

Done with her fingernails in a cute suite on the Ursula deck of *Happiness of the Sea,* Dee lifted the filthy cotton-ball mass, using her thumb and forefinger like pincers, then ditched it. She didn't ask herself where all the trash went. Into the ocean? Dee wasn't that concerned a citizen. Nor was she very mom-ish anymore, either. Mom-ing she had left behind a while ago, and her younger son, Randy, had in the last year peeled off. Her older son had gotten bored with her since his divorce and the onset of his middle age. Women could just go suck eggs.

Dee blew on her nails, smirking at them. They were a tasteful, pearly, raw chicken color.

Her sister came out of the cramped bathroom and Dee said, "Okay, they're about dried."

She recalled bathing and changing Jenny and laying her down in her bassinet for a nap.

They'd been docked for over an hour, but Dee liked to dawdle, a habit that had infuriated her dead Doug, whose presence she only sometimes missed (yet when she did, it was intolerable). He'd taken care of her, never letting her starve or go in rags. He'd bought her a Mercedes coupe. Doug had never ignored her. Dee had housebroken him to sweep and take out the trash. She had made herself his princess. He never went into debt, even for a mortgage, and he expected the rest of the country to do the same. Doug was white and had college and had gotten in at a good time, when being white with college got you a job. Doug had a gay son but opposed gay marriage. He didn't always make sense. The incoming president was a failed manager, a billionaire who ran all his vendors and creditors into debt, but Doug had kept several of those red hats, which looked clunky, making no sense—although Dee still had one she'd worn whenever they'd gone out together. It was a cheap thrill, living where they lived, which was Tennessee. The hat was a red surrender flag of sorts, a last gasp.

Then again, Doug liked to test and humiliate her, and *see* her wearing that goddamn hat.

"I don't see what the hurry is now," Jenny said cutely, closing the skinny bathroom door.

How old was Jenny? Fifty-nine. Making Dee sixty-seven. Deceased Doug would have been sixty-eight on

Saturday. The dates had just worked out. Dee and Jenny were on their way to Puerto Rico, a month before the year anniversary of his death. (Imagine dying one month to the day after your last birthday.) Doug had been unconscious—smacked-out on painkillers and anti-anxieties, not even aware of the extent of his untimely end. But it was about to be a year, a whole year. So she and Jenny were going to party. Not just celebrate but get wild.

Dee was nuts enough to think a woman her age still had it in her to get wild, but up until a couple years ago she and Doug had been getting away with it. They'd done it for scores. And then the stroke, the dementia, the brain cancer, the diapers, a drugged-out Doug talking about the present like it was the sixties again, and Doug not recognizing Dee or their older son. Had it not been for her sister, Jenny. Had it not been for faith. Had it not been for the Moscato sold in jugs.

She and Jenny baby-talked a lot, probably 90 percent of the time.

"Ou bout red-dee, Soos?"

"I bout red-deee, Soos!"

Any other sister team would have sickened from the whole act. But they enjoyed it.

They could be childlike, as tight as a jar of the jam they used to make from scuppernong, a wild grape that after it was canned looked dully gold and brackish but tasted royal and sweet.

They were living in Germantown together, eleven miles from where they'd grown up in north Memphis as fairly hard-shell Baptists. Starting with the first of her three marriages, Jenny had gone on to become a Methodist, but now she was drinking again. Three-quarters into Jenny's first piña colada, Dee would get up and go over to prop Jenny back up. Already, Jenny would be smirking at the chips. That was Dee's signal, the general smile that became the smirk at a basket of chips. Decades before, Jenny was anorexic, or else a bulimic with her finger down her throat.

They'd driven down to the Orlando/Melbourne area to look up old friends and to stay in a condo one night before climbing aboard *Happiness of the Sea* in nearby Port Canaveral. I will confess: I don't know, no one knows, what exactly happened. Dee's body would be found in the Sequester Inn Suites, between Searstown on one side and a vape emporium occupying a former Wendy's and a sandals outlet in an old Goodyear tire store in a second strip mall on the other. It was just at the moment when Tropical Storm Stella, whirling and brewing out in the Atlantic east of Puerto Rico, was about to be upgraded to Hurricane Stella. It was that distracted moment when some were worried about their property while the rest, busy having fun, were unaware of it or weren't prepared to think anything about it at all. Officially, so far there were no preparations.

The major maelstrom was days away. It wasn't an earthquake and ignorance was bliss.

Jenny's presumed body, never recovered, was seen being tossed off the stern of the Ariel deck as *Happiness of the Sea* steamed toward Vieques later in the same evening of Dee's murder.

Eric, the South African national tasked with closing the waterslide attraction The Kraken (rising snakily above the stern) was the only witness, but it was dusk. *That is definitely a body,* Eric thought as he looked out from the highest point of The Kraken, where the jets (now turned off) gushed and set you in motion. It was wrapped in a blanket or bed covering, but its shape was a body. Eric was saving to move to Australia. There were too many problems back home, racial ones, economic ones, yet whites were what the old country and the *next* country had in common. Great white sharks, not like the wankers down here—bull sharks, blacktips, reefs, hammerheads. You could end up on the chewing end of any one of them, but a white was three hideous meters of instantly constipating, shit-in-your-mouth terror. A lorry in your face, a Boko Haram ambush. Hammerheads with their eyes dorking left and right, hard to take seriously. But great whites: no. Eric would sooner swim a ten-kilometer crawl in the Gulf Stream at midnight than wade a meter into the vast and treacherous Indian. A nursery of terror—a pitch and violently claiming zone.

He'd radioed the purser when no one at the steering house or the bridge had answered. It was first seating down in three of the main dining areas, Crabby Louie's, the Castaway Grill, and the upscale Le Poisson, which is where the captain would dine every night, inviting distinguished passengers to join him at his table so they could eat the rich, bloody coq au vin of his native Gaul. As for the captain, he lived for the sea. What a pleasurable duty to have an emergency at sea and call the US Coast Guard (this was still in territorial waters): "Call up the bridge, tell them to kill the hengines, tell them to drop hanchor!" and sniffling, buttered his toast with a dab of foie gras.

IT'S ALWAYS A thrill, an up-pulse, to return. It's always necessary, the only antidote to rock fever besides weed and drink, to pick up and leave. This escape was more desperate. Now going back to Key West, going home, is proof of the cure's efficacy. His breathing. He gets off the Embraer 190, nimbly descending from the fuselage, a visceral *ahh* thrilling through him and recalibrating a wobbly heartrate. It's early evening; in the plane, as they banked and his wing dipped, clearing his steep view of the island and the town clothing it, the sun set on the lyrically incinerating expanse of liquid glass and quivering cat's paws beyond the cruise ship docks. The Gulf and the Atlantic sparkled as turquoise shaded into silvery green. And they'd gulped into their descent closer and closer to tin roofs of the old-fashioned town platting, parking lots, and steeples. It never failed to quicken him and make him thank the God he didn't believe in—except at this moment—that he'd left the money hustle and five a.m. reckonings of New York. He had no children, no attachments but friends. He had no family. He'd bugged out of that fucking situation, but *good,* after the last election cycle. Saying good-bye to parents and brother, cousins and aunts and uncles and nieces and nephews spread up and down the effing seaboard. Always this moment of landing was more salubrious even than that grand release. With each new return from visiting the old crew of familiars, Randy was new.

The sea and sky had this medicinal value, panacea or placebo indifferent. The proof was in a longer life, longer days. He was supposed to be dead seventeen years ago, but the drugs had saved him. He was a materialist but with imagination, hearing the poetry of health. His mother, gone-ass from his life, had prayed over this shit. Randy did figures . . . *I'm an accountant. I do people's taxes. I line up their earnings and weigh them against a column of deductions. There's no gray area in taxes, between the laws and the software. And it's really a wonderful scam, how quickly the workday goes. Punch in the clients' numbers, hit Save.* His days are so long. That's what he catches himself telling others. He's active at St. James Episcopal, the liberal church on Center where he helps sweep and collects the piddling tithes. He doesn't believe in any of it, of course, but he likes the good works. The city is overrun with the homeless (it is tacky to say, too Trumpish). But he will stay to midnight in the shelter distributing blankets and washing pots and pans in the dorms and soup kitchen. The rot you see on people's bodies, the scooped-out eyes of poverty. For some reason, distantly, he loves them all. The vanity of small differences; what his parents—his mother—turned their nose up at: *Keep things nice. Things not so nice, turn away.*

It's a lie about Protestants. They actually secretly love Catholics. Saints are those people who do the back work and heavy lifting so you don't have to. Pity the saintless Protestants, who are supposed to shoulder and share the work, demonstrate their faith, exemplify grace itself.

He lives in a houseboat, dry-docked in the middle of a respectable neighborhood. When the waters rise, so will the houseboat. Has a roommate. The roommate is rarely around, and the houseboat was featured in *House & Garden*. It's quaint, it's cute. Dark here, tightly lit there.

Some facts. The houseboat was moved to this slice of plot when Hurricane Wilma struck down an already delicate old wood-frame, just with its storm-surge powers. The media reported that most voters for the Mango Mussolini were poor, lower-middle-class white voters, but in fact most of his voters earned just above the line of Hillary voters. The median worth in this part of town, for instance, is one and a half million, due to the real estate values alone, whether or not it was a plumber and his family who owned. Here he was worth a lot less than a grocery manager or plumber or landscaping company owner. He was surrounded. But he'd never look back. He had decided on this instinctually, turned his back on family even before the great white tantrum.

Weirdly, Randy's one with the self-selecting refugee rednecks and bitter nonconformists.

Great white tantrum. National hissy fit. Nationalist shit fit.

The houseboat is not exactly seaworthy, but dry-docked like this it serves beautifully. Javi, the owner, pretends making it more seaworthy will be his big project, if not for retirement (that queen will never retire, he loves being needed). Javi started off in set design and window dressing and can swing a hammer. "It'll be ready for the *big bish*," Javi says about the Category 5 that might suck all this away, but he rarely comes down from New York to work on *The Magdalena*. "You never know, I might just kick over the traces, go AWOL sometime. It's just, I love what's killing me."

The *big bish*.

Javi comes from Spain. His quick conversational translations sound purplishly off-kilter.

Randy has neither Javi's sense of drama nor martyrdom-grade work ethic.

I'm a placeholder. I always was. I'm lonely, at times, but I'm wanted, and that's me too.

The tranche of property is lovely. Verdure came back with a vengeance, even exotics.

Here, he can pretend that differences don't matter, while running from small differences.

A relationship where everything was fine when in fact he wanted someone a bit younger?

A little bit prettier, but only a little bit. But new and fresh, that's all. And what else.

He's denying his childhood. It's instinctual, a survival, evolving out of the Biblical norm of Judeo-Christian super-stitions that hold together a tribe: norms, crowd control, the supernatural.

He wonders if Javi—a fashionable, if overworked, player in New York society (who also should've died and collects a modest monthly check)—cares about anything but the property. It is worth more than the structure, the slice. Only the sliver of sand and coral rock in the middle of Key West is worth something, before the Big One—and after, if the island doesn't all wash away.

The houseboat means nothing, although when he's here he goes on Grindr and the other sex-dredging apps. When it storms this structure rocks on its landlubber mooring. It's a magical feeling, sex and the feeling of Robert Louis Stevenson dry-docked but holding fast, waiting for a flood, the storm surge that is inevitable. People don't want to talk about it in the Trump era, the Mango Mussolini who gives meaning to the disparity in America, the difference between what's real and what's abject, obscene, morally filthy. Between what should be and what shall never be.

In the hypothetical theme, a rusty harmonica whine into a silvery Dobro slide.

He used to love people, lovers and family and exes. He's no longer thus encumbered.

He told the others sharing his last name to go fuck themselves and never call him again.

They obeyed! Morons.

You belong with a lover, like a riotous tropical plant, a vine. Be a strong-rooted lover, a tree. Be the one who supports, upholds. Be the one who cares. Though you may no longer care.

This is the last ditch gorgeously enclimbed with flowering vines. The bougainvillea, the trumpet-flowers, the pitcher-blooms, the up-gasping blossoms that last a fortnight, lovely nights. A night-blooming garden, here in this garden that helps describe the utopia of the night, a heaven.

(Sip of chalky, dark red wine.)

Dark and plumbed by sin, suddenly bright in patches and whorls, the blooms of evening.

(Another sip.)

The bloom-spots, the ghosts of midnight or else pre-morning, the denizens of pale gloom.

Moon-brights, star-furls, scent-spots, quick and almost undetectable, a dim squint-garden.

(*And may my love travel with you always,* he thought foolishly but only to never-hads.)

Solitude germinated them, loneliness made them effloresce shyly while no one watched.

DEE AND JENNY began at Margaritaville, obviously. They snacked on appetizers, the Onion Loaf, the Lava Lava Shrimp, most important, the Conch Fritters. They stopped ordering before Volcano Nachos. No entrées. Very prissily, Dee's son had once advised her before he left her life forever that entrée in French actually meant appetizer. Dee was not ashamed to be American. The word for her was *American.* She knew this because she'd been using it her whole life. She was eleven when she took her mother's generally unconsulted *Betty Crocker Cookbook* down from the shelf and read, knitted her brows, and got a ballpoint pen and paper. A different planet. She wanted a kitchen and hearth that welcomed the people her future husband had over from work. She willed a home (*I'll be a homemaker . . .* she'd never really wanted to work longer than she had to), and it had nice things to make things easier, cozier. Trays and platters for rows and circles of nibbles that she passed around, fielding compliments, laughing demurely, her eyelashes like coal-dusty moths, flutter-flutter: "Well all it is, is Betty Crocker. You think I'm some durn gourmet?"

The photo colors were in strange inks, the kitchens and dining rooms jellied, jaundiced.

"Dee. *Do tell.* How on earth do you get these so moist?"

And she'd gotten there. But entertaining mostly was for relatives or the boss once a year.

She found that making and keeping friends was hard and anxious-making and finally sad.

She'd learned from her family how to make friends. It was like being friendly in church. And it was the church, the congregation, that exerted the pressure that held folks together. But in real life there was nothing so set and permanent that kept people together. Their differences, *even the small ones,* grated. In church it was agreed, everybody agreed, Christ was their savior. It held marriages together. It didn't have to echo a whole lot, or be defined or explained, it just was.

In their last few years alive together, she and Doug would skip dinner and eat popcorn. It was an annoying thought, dragging out the groceries and cookware. There was a sell-by date on everything: the food, the memory of wanting to do it, of taking possible pleasure in doing it. The dishes after, the wiping-up, the sanitizing, remembering to include the sponge in the dishwasher.

Jesus was busy with younger families elsewhere; he was really overstretched, that Christ.

She'd felt Him in the presence of her boys, even when she was anxious, down, and sad.

They'd always been in a hurry at the table. Dee wasn't sure she had a lot to say. What a relief, actually, when the boys finally moved out. She might pause doing a task, straightening a closet. She might stare, adjust her glasses. But why, in order to better see what?

She might catch herself before starting to cry, but usually she didn't cry.

They'd breakfasted on the ship then skipped lunch. Margaritaville, Margaritaville!

A dark minute: she remembered the road trips of the seventies with Doug and their sons. Side of the road, Stuckey's to pee and fill up on snacks, lunch itself not necessary. Butterscotch milkshakes, saltwater taffy, and, her favorite, peanut brittle, playing hell on her bridgework. The dentistry of the time: gold crowns, making Doug recoil at the bills. But neither side of the family had been blessed with good teeth. Past way gone, but it was pretty to recall. On now.

A blues band called the Rubber Brothers was setting up and the sisters were out of there. Jenny left half a frozen strawberry margarita, the baskets of snacks half consumed. It got louder.

Dee said, "I don't know about you, baby girl, but I'm ready to get right-wild!"

The idiom, the Southern idiocy, the lunacy of feeling special, cute little differences, trivia.

They proceeded down Duval, that magical, claustrophobic, vomit-alley venue.

Lights, noise, pushing-shoving, she'd had just enough tequila to deal with this.

Behind it, a feeling of cute menace. Doug would love this. He'd choogle and shout.

He'd get celebratory, seized by sudden joy, going against that old Baptist primness.

Doug could dance him up some. No one got on top of Doug, in terms of getting wild.

Then upstairs at the 801, drag show. Actually, Jenny had never attended a drag show—if *attended* was the right word. She knew RuPaul, but who didn't? Dee would happily be her guide. Back when they were whole, the nuclear family convened here for long weekends. The last road trip with the boys, actually, was that. Before the ugly metaphorical flood. Before the country turned itself inside-out saltily, near-bloodily.

Doug had been sick the first time but was rallying. The troops. Joe's kids; Randy and his boyfriend at the time. There was some hope. They'd be a family again, although Randy had said, "Mom, Joe and I were never like brothers. All he ever did was push me away, I think knowing I was gay. Don't you understand? Where we're from, queer's bad. It's still bad, and I don't ever want to go back. I'm glad to see y'all. But I hate where we're from. I'm not a proud local son."

"I'm sorry to hear that."

She was really naive, wasn't she? It was automatic words popping out.

Well, Randy always had that kind of poetic flourish, but she got it now. This was here at a guesthouse some years ago. His reckoning had chilled her; Randy meant business, not fucking around anymore. She had to sit up straight and listen. There was no Trump then, he wasn't even a thing. Not the remotest possibility, sweet innocence. She remembered cracking open a Miller.

And for some reason, Dee remembered her father dying in a hospital in Jackson. He was an elder at Sunshine Baptist, and God that name. He read the Bible every day but was furious he was dying—so unjust! Presented a little black ledger of accounts, what each of her siblings had taken, what was owed in the will, what had been sub-tracted for brothers who'd run into the law.

Divorces, tax evasion, pot dealing. They were supposed to be respectable but were not.

"Feel angry," old Wayne said, "betrayed. Thought I had a good ten years ahead of me."

The Goodyear electrician had recently retired. Loved tending to his vegetable garden.

Grew tomatoes. An acre of lettuce, tomatoes, squash, string beans, sweet wet melons.

"Mad at God," he'd moaned and sort of sung, the man who couldn't sing, caterwauling from his throne near the choir, an awful holler. "I'm mad at God. Mad at God. Mad at God."

The Gospels said to take in the sick and poor, but at the last minute Dee had flinched.

She hadn't lost everything, but she'd lost most of it. Held her nose and pulled the lever.

I WANTED TO be your lover, but you had other things, mainly family. Your sprawling Italians by blood, siblings, nieces, nephews. Now great nieces and nephews, a handsome cohesive family. I was jealous, but I tried not to show it. This was why I asked myself how I kept coming back and back to New York and took the train to Queens. That Yemeni restaurant you took me to and paid, knowing I'd served in the Peace Corps in Yemen, the food nostalgic. Running from family—and you feeling sorry for me. Prescriptive, yet protesting you could no longer take antidepressants as the only sure cure was to be in the bosom of the people pledged to protect you for life.

Which I respected and I still do.

How I'd look and look at you.

Your seemingly congenital sadness forced at bay by your hard, sheer will.

Large, baleful, dark green eyes, and to me a head like an independent sexual organ, clipped hair, and ears like jug handles to pinch or kiss in the dark or early-early light —so I've imagined.

New York is generally a mystery to a Southerner; a giant, kind, accommodating figment.

It's not supposed to be. It's supposed to be merciless, outsized and cold, crushing down. I love it, but I decided to come down here for peace of mind, though I miss you. I miss your left-eyebrow-up smirk. Your gravelly hush-voice, your long legs never in shorts. A soft hoot-voice.

How beautiful you are, a child in middle age, five o'clock shadow against the baby mug.

New York: Woody Allen movies, all the books and movies about it.

And your career, and now your fiancé. He is your age and perfect for you. He worships you, which is meet and right as the Bible goes; the first blush of affection that becomes true love.

THIS WEATHER. I keep thinking of music where the storm is sucked into the burning atmosphere, in order to wash it out, the pull and swell and explosion and spread. The soggy air getting wetter and unbearably thicker. I keep thinking of Steppenwolf's "Magic Carpet Ride," where the Hammond B-3 owns the song's landscape, thunder here and there, distant, becoming a moan that becomes a hoof-hum that gathers in pillow concussions like sections of hot dusty electrical front that move in herd-like, the herd of sound surrounding yet almost comfortingly, the business of the storm going on in apparently thin air, columns of draft, warm earth and surface, cool swirling winds striking heat, friction and moisture, turbulence, all of it apparently unseen until it's too late although to be fair there are the signs: the rising barometric pressure, the general bodily unease, a feeling of craziness, discomfort, irritability, horniness, morbidity, preoccupation with death, love.

GETTIN' WILD, MISSION approaching accomplished.

The drag venue's filling up, they get a table not far from the stage. Jenny's been through three marriages, one-two-three, the last sticking for the longest but ending seemingly forever ago. An air force captain retiring at the end as a lieutenant colonel, but they were toast by then. Well, she has the two kids—and grown, they make her proud. Well, more the grandkids. Jenny thinks, *I'm less alone than Dee, and still it's not enough. I have an addiction, my real addiction's things. I see three-four things I need and snatch them all up and use my card and take them home to look at them longer and further up-close, and start saying, "No. No. Maybe. Yes." And I don't mind at all, I will stand in line at the Returns for upward of forty-five minutes assured I had plenty of time to brood things over, although I've gotten faster at it. And don't usually miss out on a thing. I raised my two kids bringing things home that way, bags of this stuff, so they didn't have to drag along and get on my nerves. Getting kids to try things on. Well, the captain and I spoiled them. Now I have the grandkids to dress, and because we don't all live together, the process takes longer. Though they don't appreciate the clothes as much.*

They ask you for money. They ask for a new car.

But it's more pitiful with Dee, who's lost about everyone.

She never lost through divorce. To me she was always Doug's princess. She didn't have time, or luck, you might put it, to learn about losing. Things were smooth sailing for, like, ever.

Dee could've stood to lose somebody here and there along the way. Divorce doesn't kill.

Oh, it burns, it scars. But you're still alive.

I'M ABOUT FIVE seconds out the door and on the ladder, getting landlubbered, when I see the Kid. *The Kid!*, who was supposed to leave town and get out of my hair forever. I do not want to have sex with this guy; I do not find him attractive. He's getting off his jalopy bike with difficulty, his fat ass hitching this way, and slopping that. Albeit still a youth, sort of, a guy like this should not wear shorts or T-shirts. He's awkward, shifting, bike frame jerking away from him. He stops as though feral, yet, and I hate to say it but it's true, Drew has no reliable animal instincts, he's not even that basic. His limbic system is burnt out from the frazzled rewiring of abuse. He's polite, I will give him that, but boy is he dumb, enough to think I lust him just because he's under thirty.

He doesn't even hear my feet on the deck. *Moron.*

To witness him loading carbohydrates and greasy starches into an underaccommodating mouth, one that was obviously meant to suckle at Mom's teat a while longer, is to want to barf lunch. And he won't do himself the favor of eating vegetables. It's mashed potatoes and gravy, gummy pasta. A Coke! Who, anymore, drinks Coke? Or even a Coke Zero? Who gets all their therapy from eating obviously unhealthy, shitty, snack-like, gut-buster garbage pickings—worse than dumpster diving for morsels? Christian evangelicals fucked him up, and the kidnappers did nearly worse. (Never got the full story on the kidnapping and I would far from blame the victim, and I don't think he's made it up, but to ask him to tell me would no doubt be tedious and like an unnerving stroll across ground you think's mined, because he can never choose the shortest route to recounting his tale.) All because, and I know this is wrong to say, but I'm only thinking it, this here Drew is too goddamn dumb and trusting; he obviously hasn't learned from his trauma at the hands of patently terrible crocodilian people but also cagey nerds like me who resent obligations and pile them on themselves nonetheless—all because forty years ago some Southern subdivision queen decided she needed a best friend, a baby to raise her—well, maybe neither of us in fact has learned anything. But really, chit in my column: I never had to ask for an open-ended loan.

But then I think, Oh my god I was just like that once, that was me. And I cringe innerly.

He's not yet at the honeysuckle-covered gate. I hear a rattle of heavy bike chain, perfect idget. Who wants your rusted-out beater? The chain is worth more than that wreck, dipshit.

Can I just please sneak back up the ladder, without the boat rocking audibly, get back into the cabin, and lock up shop from inside? Like, I don't even give a shit if he hears, as long as I'm inside without him looking at me with his repulsively stricken squinters and worse, a weirdly wet, lusty, upcurving lip. He doesn't dump his innuendo on me live, though, he puppy-beams; but that little bitch is an overfed, aging-out whelp. He saves his horny notions for texts, and *please* name me one thing more passive than a millennial, where all is accomplished by fingertip and then the phone repocketed. Waits. Gets the tit- or thigh-buzz, slides it back out. All afternoon long back and forth. News flash: I do not want to keep tracking your cute follow-up remarks and annoying emojis! In truth, I should thank you for driving me to power down my device completely. For a while I got no peace, twerp kept writing me until he decided to move on, returning to Brooklyn.

"Randy! Hey, buddy! Hey Randy!"

I turn. I'm that silly goose again—I respond, the way I responded once on Facebook. I'd just posted eleven miles of rage against the presidential administration. I got friended God knows how since I'd never heard of him and I got Drew for my pains. *Never do that again.*

"Hi, Drew," I call drily. "I thought you were permanently gone. Why are you back?"

"Funny story. I'll tell you in a minute. Can I come up?"

"My roommate is here. Let's go someplace else."

"Oh. Okay."

At the Bottle Cap two blocks away, Drew is mopping his forehead, finding some damn place under the table to set his overburdened backpack, which for all I know contains all of his worldly effects, or the most portable ones. He's told me he has things in storage in Virginia, his books, his professional clothes. He's worked in IT all over the country and has the amazing ability to find jobs at companies that were always about to close in another two or three months.

But there was freedom in instability, and enlightenment, he said.

How I loathe the E-word, and plus, I see no evidence of that quality in Drew, at all.

There were no IT jobs in Key West. I'd told him he had to work in hospitality, which is the only industry around here. Wait tables, work at a tourist or gay establishment of some kind.

Make some commitment. I can't help it, I didn't make the rules. It's a gig economy.

He'd lollygagged. I knew those jobs—if shitty, if humiliating, if hectic, and degrading and overexhausting—were plentiful. He'd put in a few applications then took off from the shelter overnight to go back to Brooklyn. Texted me the news from the Greyhound bus on the Overseas Highway. That feeling of relief, and freedom. But I was a fool to think I'd gotten rid of him that fast, I now see. He's ordered the messiest sandwich the Bottle Cap serves— ham, sauerkraut, and Swiss with Russian dressing on toasted rye, a Red Baron—and is not aware of the rude spectacle watching him attempt to hold the (What is it, it's no longer food, because who would eat it, since it resembles more a crime scene?)—of course, he's ordered the messiest sight ever presented the viewer. I feel sorry for him, I do, but good lord.

But it's never more than ten minutes before one of his offhanded—no, keen—reminders.

He escaped those evangelicals. He briefly attended a bible college, while his high school boyfriend (the two sets of parents had attempted to separate them like Romeo and Juliet) went to another across the state line in North Carolina. Long story short, the boyfriend succumbed to the needs of Christ and a community of Christians who had his higher spiritual needs in mind.

In Brooklyn, Drew found his new community: hipsters and gender-vagues, queers, fluids, grown "theybies," religious refugees like himself, young people too frightened to identify at all.

But he still had to make a living. All while dealing with his all-enslaving trauma.

Never even suspected, is how he presents it. *Caught up, entangled, spat out, shit out.*

Boy does have a lyrical way, though, of sorts. If he could just quit perseverating.

Undigested by upbringing, crudely shuttled along the entrails of Judeo-Christian concepts and symbolic shibboleths of the stubborn fundamentalist, Drew came out the other end unrefined by any point of view. They hadn't been able to protect him from the media, they had drunk their own Kool-Aid. I know this about myself. I'm Drew's parents' age. We like our attachments. It would take a lot to change their minds about anything they hold dear, because they always held it dear. I just happen in middle age to disagree with them entirely. But I reach for things, too.

I got out luckier, I get it. I gulped the nightmare and proceeded with a little luck. I'd had luck, and my family were the milder form of Southern post-redneck Christian bigot. Hoodless.

And there's the fact that everything added up has made Drew totally nuts. I chose to drink.

"Not *one,*" he says, "in my family will admit to spiritual doubt. That itself is a sign."

"I don't doubt that. You haven't met a lot of my family."

"I don't want to get into your family. I don't know them."

"I don't know yours."

"Will you listen? Will you just listen to me?"

"You're going in," I say. "You're going to that place where you vote not to be reached."

"Ha ha. I need you to be smarter than that. Okay, Randy?"

I say, "I'm so tired. I can't get dragged into the whirligig wake of your obsessions."

"Obsessions? These are valid experiences. Personal, real-ass experiences, Randy."

"I don't doubt that, in your mind. But you and I've gone all through all of them before."

Napkin-dabbing his mouth, Drew says, "I just need a little more support, not a lot."

"Okay," I say. "Let's back up, start over as it were. Why did you come back here?"

"I couldn't stay up there. The winter's too long. I'm not used to that. And I don't know anybody anymore. They've all moved up; they've all moved on. They're, like, in offices now and they have their own apartments and have mortgages, and they have cars they have to garage, and they're having kids and suddenly they decide they hate their peeps who're losers, and they've—"

"Drunk the Kool-Aid," I supply.

Drew puts down his sandwich calmly saying, "Yeah man, exactly. How did you know?"

"I know because I've been listening. I don't think you're making excuses. But you need to plant yourself in some soil that's fertile. You need to find where that's best. A place, pick it."

"I think it's got to be here," he says. "Everybody's weird here, you're weird but so am I."

"I think you need to pick a place less nutty, decide on it, and stay there, put down roots. I think you need to quit uprooting and landing somewhere and asking for money to be wired."

"I heard you, Jesus Christ. Jesus fucking Christ, Randy. So this is about money."

"Which I'm not made of," I say, nodding.

Drew says, "But I never wanted it to be about money!"

"But you kept asking for it!"

"What do you think I am, a prostitute?" he says.

"God no, man. Oh, God no."

"You think I'm not good enough to be a call boy, or a rent boy, whatever your generation said. You boomers or Xers or whatever you are are all the same. You think I couldn't make it as a hooker? A sex worker? You have no faith or imagination. You're saying I'm too smart."

I wait and then I say, "I'm not saying that at all."

"What are you saying?"

"I'm saying, I'm asking, have you gone back to St. James and asked for a cot?"

"I have done that very freaking thing."

"Good," I say. "And?"

"And they don't have one for me. There's too many others in even worse shape."

"What really happened up there?" I then ask him. "You weren't really gone that long."

"What happened, Randy, is I couldn't even get a fucking couch to surf on, okay? Not one of my friends would help me out, so I guess the next thing I need to do is get new friends."

"Getting friends," I say, putting my thoughts together, "doesn't sound nearly as urgent to me as it might seem to you. I'm talking about a job, a place to stay, some fucking money."

"Thank you for clarifying," he says. "So it is about money, it's about conveniences and things that are convenient for you. Randy, I'm looking at you, and I'm looking at you . . ."

He pushes back the revolting evidence from the crime scene he's given up interest in.

He has a maddening flair, his words at times racing out of his mouth, manipulatingly.

"And what?" I say.

". . . and I keep looking at you."

"I see you, too, Drew."

"And I'm trying to decide, *Is this a friend?* I want to see the good in you, just temporarily a good person. I won't even go so far as to say the Christ in you, which is what my mom says."

"Fuck your mom."

"That's what I say. But it's still worth considering. When that man got me tweaked, and got me naked, and I was too tweaked to do anything, and he started wrapping me in duct tape—"

"I'm not even sure that happened, Drew, actually."

"Google it! He left me in the ghetto in Philly. It was interstate! A federal crime!"

"Okay, I believe you. And I believe in—"

"Trauma! I've come through a life of trauma."

My heart does respond with pangs.

"I know, I know."

He's revolting and repulsively clueless, but that's no excuse for universal cruelty. Jesus, I hate religion. Greed is responsible for half of this, and religion picks up the check for the rest.

He starts to cry but then stops and sucks up the snot and says, "I just need one friend."

"And I need you to have a plan, just not another sudden move."

"You were dying for me to move."

"To be honest, I was dying for it not to be my problem anymore."

"That's the whole problem with your generation. That's why we have Trump. Laziness. Your generation didn't want to do anything radical or new," he says, and he's got me there. We were waiting for a miracle that was set to arrive, all by itself somehow, but protesting wasn't our suit, not yet. And he goes on, "If you're going to talk the talk. You know I'm right ideologically."

"Your generation didn't come out to vote. That's statistical. Half the rest voted stupidly."

"I'm not going to kill myself," he says. "That's not in my disorder, that's another one."

There was a time, there was a time . . .

But that's the same thinking as the Mango Mussolinis. That's their nostalgia, not mine.

I'm queer. I hate hometowns. I love socialism. Give me socialism and a decent place to live, and give this kid one, too, and teach him to learn how to love dishwashing for a little while.

I did plenty of dishwashing in my time—which is true, but fuck, just listen to me.

WE'RE IN THE middle of the first show, just sitting, watching—up comes a girl, a young woman.

"Excuse me, are these two places at your table taken?"

"They're not," says Jenny, and I could just about kill her.

"Hi, I'm Amber! This is an Amber Alert, ha ha!"

That gets us laughing, the pictures on the milk cartons.

"This is Pete, and we're a duo. Best friends."

Pete: "I'm here, I'm queer, get used to it!"

Our father would probably come right out and say, "Hi, neighbor!" Wouldn't even think about it. Took his faith to heart. Our mother would have sniffed and held off being the bossy one, waiting to say she told him so. It didn't usually need to be said. He won out with good-natured charity. Charity was his thing, what I wish I'd taken more to heart. I am hard like my mother, who taught me, while my father showed me. I'm tipsy enough to smile.

Goll-darn, I miss him. I miss the time when I should have paid more attention to him. I wonder what he'd say about these weird, funny Wonder Twins.

Amber is pretty but with some mileage on her; Pete is handsome. We can barely hear them through the music, but then the Cher act is done and they sit down and start right in.

Pete says, "How are y'all? Having a good time?"

We say we're having a good time, and Jenny is half in the bag, so she doesn't care.

Jenny says, adjusting her voice less mousily, "Nice to meet y'all. Where you from?"

"Oh God!" they both say, falling about in their chairs, all of us grinning.

I don't know what it is. It's old summers. Something about them reminds me of the past. Of my brother, Jenny's and my baby brother. This pains me, and I need to fetch better memories, since I don't want to believe the things— can't believe—the things Randy told me about Benjy.

We settle right in, and I think, I could just die happily now, thinking about my Douglas.

I'd just love to tell them about Doug, about how fun they'd think he was. Then boom.

I'm recalling the wheelchair ritual, how I took him I don't know how many times into the emergency room when he talked and didn't make sense, or when he collapsed. He'd insisted on me driving him even though we could afford the ambulance. With all our money, how I'd saved, cut corners. They did a scan, they checked him out without saying it was serious, and then when we left he had to be pushed out to the curb for me to pick him up. Like he was this liability. And what does insurance mean. Everybody's worried about a lawsuit. He was treated like trash to be deposited outside hospital grounds. And the nurses and the staff, so lazy and unconcerned about my husband. It was me. I got increasingly angry. It was me getting upset about Medicare: What good is something you pay into all your life when you're not going to be treated decently? Like a human being who paid into a system that was supposed to take care of you, and not cheap. When they found the spot in his lung and he went in for surgery and the black attendant pushing him into the room to be operated on said, "Smoker, coming through. Smoker!" Now is that racist?

A couple of times, before the tumors sapped his breath, then the new ones fuzzied up his thinking—there were a couple of times when they wheeled him out of the hospital lobby before I trotted off to get the car, and Doug tore up the porte-cochère in his wheelchair, whirling, rolling, popping wheelies, the way he'd never let go in a real car, only on a dance floor, because safety first.

But after that initial burst, he'd be slumped, fit to be dead back home, looking lonely.

Baby brother Benjy is next, it's happening. Cigarettes, and no one gets out of that one.

Jenny's the one who did diaper duty on little Benjamin. I was cooking.

We deserve this little reprieve, this cruise and vacation. We need magic.

Benjy was the hot-rodder in my family. He was too young and carefree and all the ladies' man to touch Randy, or get the idea even. He was sixteen, and for him babysitting was a gas. He loved kids and wanted them and that's why he ended up having three. Getting mixed up in drugs was his only sin and mistake, marijuana, new girls his vice. He admits all that last part now. But he doesn't have to own up to that horrible stuff Randy accused him of, and why should he? Randy is angry, and bitter, and the election didn't go his way. And things are getting worse for him now. I miss him but how silly, how dodo, can you be? Unable to own up to your failings in your career, who lost some years, maybe, or never quite got all the love. I sometimes hate him.

That saves me, my sense of proportion. I had two sons and did the best I could.

I used to wait for the sun to go down, except in the summer when it felt like it wouldn't.

But now I just have a little Moscato any old time I feel like it.

Amber says, "What are you ladies up to tonight? Making a hop off one of the ships?"

Jenny says, "We're on *Happiness of the Sea,* and it is lovely. It is *nice,* girl!"

Strangers have a good effect on her, turns out. That's from being a military wife, I'd bet.

I nod. I've applied thick black wings like the girls are doing these days, making their eyes look surprised and a little funky, like in the sixties. I think I'm cute.

There's no age anymore! We say "girl" and "baby girl" and nobody frets a forehead.

"You hear that, Pete? She says the ship is lovely. Feed you right, give you lots of things to do? Diverting activities? Y'all like gambling? Slot machines? Blackjack? Oh, yum."

Jenny says, "I do have a weakness for slot machines. I love me some slot machines."

It's true, Jenny's a gambling addict, always in the car pointed down to Mississippi.

Pete says, "There's nothing wrong with slot machines. You say y'all are from Memphis, so does that mean you've been down to Tunica, done the riverboat gambling?"

Amber says, "See, we're from around those parts. Pascagoula, Jackson—"

We brighten. Southerners can really get together and hee-haw us something fierce.

THERE IS A thing in the South—the gift of the gab, the law of the desert. Welcoming. I am just about all over it, but I can feel myself sliding into it. I don't love this kid, but I feel sorry for him.

I don't even like head. I'll give it for a few minutes then get bored, and getting it doesn't do anything for me. It tickles, irritates. Looking at his formless, gormless mouth, I'm imagining telling him to go down on my dick while calling him a faggot and a piece of shit. He'd eat it up. I'd get something out of it, too. I'd get him to shut the fuck up and get some control over him; I'd feel good later about telling him more pointedly his ideas are unconsidered. But Drew's not too dumb, survivors can't be. So dorky and misshapen; needs to put that highly verbal mouth to work—taken down a peg. I'd then turn over and make him feast on my crack and hole if he ever wants another Red Baron. What happens when the novelty wears off, how to get rid of a slave?

I'm on my third beer.

Drew says, "I didn't tell you about the sharks, how my boyfriend who runs a tourist boat, just for fun, will hook a shark and for the amazement of the passengers will fuck with it. I think he's a real sadist, but clinically speaking a narcissist. I've been reading about that. He needs the attention of an audience. The tourists here are like the people back home, just trash. Anything'll amuse them. He keeps it hooked and gets the motor going and drags it behind the boat, and they love it. People have no feeling. They're numbed. They're numbed to the world all around them and whatever amusement strikes their fancy, and they've been drinking; they love that shit."

Decreasingly, incrementally less, moronic. I notice I'm starting to nod.

I dare: "What happens to the shark?"

"I saw it once. He was really proud to show me on a video he made. I could report him, and I will if he YouTubes it. He was like, 'Watch this shit.' The shark was, I think, a blacktip, not even that big. It was a defenseless creature, with the hook in its gills."

"What a piece of shit."

"Exactly. He drags the thing at a slow speed. It's flipping and curling in the wake. Then he stops in waters he knows and waits. The other sharks come around. You can't believe how it turns them on. Not the sharks, the passengers. And they go nuts. It's sick. It's disgusting."

"They eat it, they feed on it. The other sharks, I mean."

"Like one of their own prey. Anything leaking blood. And he thinks this is a gift to me."

IT TAKES A while, but Pete opens up and gets wild and boy is it good.

He says, "Knock-knock."

We say, "Who's there?"

"No drama."

"No drama who?"

"No drama Obama."

It feels good to laugh. I'm not sure what it means, but it's about that asshole Obama.

"Can I just say," says Amber, "what a disappointment and disaster Barack Obama was?"

"You may," Jenny says, with a nervous type of laugh.

I say, because I always said cute things that I tried to make Doug laugh with, "Ew, you're saying his full name." (A joke like that's funnier, more feminine.) "Don't say his full name!"

Oh, god, I'm going to hell is a fun thought to have all the sudden.

"Excuse me, Dee," says Pete. "The former monkey in chief's full name is Barack Hussein Obama, and if you believe he was born in Hawaii or the mainland of the United States—"

We all look around at one another, showing crazy-grin teeth.

"A bridge?" I say. "In Brooklyn?"

My mother wanted me to be more demure.

"Hear, hear!"

All but Jenny. She didn't like Obama any more than we did, but she doesn't get the joke. Jenny never just went with it. She'll shut off from her corner, but she was always half a step off. She's the one who wouldn't miss Sunday school for anything, but it was just an excuse to take an hour for her hair, and she's a little bit more particular with her clothes, given lint and fit and all.

Pete says, "It's fun to meet you ladies. Amber and I don't get out that much."

I do want to ask how they make their living. I mean, what do they both do to eat?

"Y'all don't get out much?" I say. "Not even as a team? Work too hard?"

"We don't," says Amber. "It's the liberals. Have you noticed about the liberals, how full of resentment they are about our leadership? These people were democratically elected, fair and square. Let the man do his goll-dang job! They're clogging up the system, slowing progress."

"That's what I say."

"This place is loaded with liberals. I mean, not this place, but Key West."

"Amber gets carried away, but yeah. It's refreshing when you meet people you know are not going to gang up on you and start dumping that bleeding-heart liberal stuff onto your head."

"Don't get us wrong, Pete and I don't even agree on everything. But it's not because he's queer or from a different class or what have you. We care about others, much as anybody can."

"Amber, recite them some of your greeting card psalms. She writes these really killer-ass greeting card psalms. I just know with copyright rights they'll really take off, now that American people have started coming back to their damned senses. What we need is further inspiration."

Amber clears her throat humbly and says, "Be that as it may."

"Just one, honey. You're my own little Emily Dickinson. Fuck Toni Morrison!"

Amber crosses her eyes like she's trying not to cut a smelly wet one and recites:

How did they come to kill my Lord?
Was it greed
Was it that old Devil
Or were they just bored?

"I love it," I say, because I do, since something about it sounds true, and all that.

Jenny says, "Now isn't that cute."

I get shot a look of "What?" from Pete, and he's handsome and so appealing, like Randy.

If only I could introduce him to Randy, I've a weird feeling they'd get on like whatever.

Pete reminds me of a young Doug. They have a similar demeanor, same sense of humor.

Never cared for gingers, but Pete's neat.

Does that all sound incestuous? I'm half in the bag already. There's a Bette Midler on.

I say, "Do y'all live down here now? I hate to sound nosy but here we are, and it's fun."

"You could say temporarily we're living here. But we do travel together, move together."

"We're the dos amigos."

"I love it!"

Jenny says, "Are they actually going to put that on Hallmarks or American Greetings?"

Jenny's drunk. You never know. Whenever we go out and I know she's going to have more than one, I make her leave her wallet with all her credit cards at home or in the room. For all I know she'd just hand over her cash and cards to complete strangers. Baby sisters need help.

A CREEPING GRACE. A lurching empathy, if it's empathy. A moral loathing has subsided, while I've still got my gut repulsion. How can I make it so that I never have to watch him eat again?

Creeping, too, is my pathological need to be alone in Noah's drydock, damned to dream.

My youthful prejudices dissolve in the air. My mind was so small and narrow, molded like it was after my parents, a few years as they were away from dirt farming in Tennessee. So ignorant. It's fun to draw your eyes up and imitate Asians. I dream, for instance, on the beautiful Korean owner of the burrito palace, whose skin is like butter the instant before it's pan-browned, and I worry, as I invoke sexual needs and feelings, orders whined and requests croaked and made direct, that I exoticize, if this harms me more than it does him, beautiful him. Endless solipsism.

But if Drew is going to stay here a few weeks—a gamble, since I'm going to take Javi the fashionista's cabin—I might send him out with money and say, *I've got work to do and I need the space alone, and do a little pavement pounding while you're at it, get some fresh air and find a place to smoke your weed, because it's crowded belowdecks and stuffy down here to begin with—and hey, knock yourself out.* Javi never comes down without letting me know a week ahead or I've never known him to. He and I have a past, and with that past the present is nailed down so the future can be of no threat. We've never fought since we broke it off, already in Paris back in that time when I still respected my family and the religiously attached people I grew up around. I was still afraid of the death I wondered if I didn't deserve. I didn't even question it, it was coming after me. Javi and I fought over money, we fought over his Catholic upbringing, we fought over atheism. Like every Protestant who loathes faith and any odor of superstition, I romanticized the Roman church. Javi and I fought over Franco and we fought over democracy, neither satisfactory to him. He'd made peace with the world's fallen state. Now with the time gone by I realize I finally must, too, but I can never be the old pretty one I was, and neither can he, although he shines beyond the need for beauty. He was my first out of college, when I took my useless humanities degree to Paris before I woke up in Javi's apartment and he began to berate me between sex. He couldn't help it and so he apologized. It was growing up poor, an only child in Murcia with only a mother, who'd made of her son the man she needed, and who induced him to beat her. Javi was used to savaging her from the age of fourteen on. Something pulled his hand up from his side—he believed in spirits, angels, and even the djinn from his distantly Moorish heritage—and looped the belt. Something raised the hand and belt in an arc over his head and yanked it into a hot viper strike. Something once it unleashed him made him want to murder her, the harder she shrieked and pled, "Don't kill me!" Made him hate her, pity himself, and then hate himself and pity her. Even then he couldn't stop. This, for some reason, gave Javi a superior air, his shame having caused him undue, unsolicited suffering.

"You don't understand what I go through, what it put me through, what she did to me."

"I do," I lied, as he deflated and cooled and calmed down. "Or I just think I do."

Then, more levelly, Javi said: "It would have been better if my people had gone to South America. It would have given us stiffer stuff. It would have made us work harder."

The only thing I like less about a man from a social democratic country is one who acts like a goddamn

Republican. Javi has always made shit up. Social democrats from the continent, I'm sorry to report, are soft and will accept or say any goddamn thing they please.

Javi sucks the teat of the generous fat-sacked State of New York and is a fucking Trumpy.

DO YOU KNOW what that's like, to be a mother and so separated? A desperation beyond reason. I am hearing that I might see my son. That's all I want, if it's possible. Just want to see Randy.

And Pete says, "I know him. He looks like you, only he's a little bit taller, right?"

"We're pretty distinctive. People always thought we were brother and sister. They called us Black Irish, but I still don't know what that means, do you? You can see I'm confused."

"I see him around town a lot now, older than me but looks good. A little skinny."

"That's him!" I say. "I think. Haven't seen him in a couple."

Jenny nods rapidly and stupidly.

"I don't want to be obnoxious, but I think we even got into a kissing match. Don't worry, he was a gentleman. He's not your regular slut. I'm not exactly a Robert Redford."

"How did you know who I was thinking of?"

"Pete gets it all the time," Amber says. "But I think I should get Jenny back to the ship."

I say, "I don't know."

"It's Friday. Everybody in Key West is at Bobby's, doing karaoke. I'll take you there."

"You really think he'll be there?"

Amber says, "Dee looks so, I don't know—she looks like she really wants to see her boy."

I never thought I'd see him again.

I say, "And I'm worried for Jenny. She's tired, needs to get back to the ship."

"Jenny's fine," says Amber. "I'll take her back to the ship and you've still got an hour. I'll get the car."

Jenny nods foolishly and says, "Go. Let's go."

Pete innocently nods fast and says, "Amber and I know somebody on the *Happiness*!"

It is already happening. We're leaving together, woozy, boozy-woozy, I'm not a girl now.

I'm thinking about Orange Beach. Doug and I are still in love. I can feel that. We're so in love nothing else matters. The boys are out at the beach. This is our one chance this week. I am so sad. Sex can be so sad, until it's what the doctor ordered. It feels dirty, and then it heals.

We wanted one more, a girl. Randy kept saying he wanted a sister.

I'm back there, when I first felt young. Only occasionally can I feel young again.

I never believed that about Jesus. Jesus was always there, about to interfere.

How do you have this hanging over your shoulder while trying to be in the world now?

I'm so frightened, and I've never been this ready. I want to be back there. I want heaven.

If you would know eternal life, come with me and fear not death. Death is never the end.

Or something like that.

BATTEN DOWN, AS they say, the hatches. A beginning, spattering rain. Maybe it's the big one.

A moment in Aigues-Mortes, Javi in his finest physical shape.

He says, "You have made my life a living hell."

I say, "I'm sorry, but I've loved you."

He looks at me with pity. How many men have enjoyed his body, just in the last week?

Time and again Javi told me, "No one loves just for love, just for who you are, Randy."

First the humidity, swelling, pressing. Then the winds, more spatters of rain on the roof.

The winds, the winds. Don't let anyone tell you to fear the rising water—the rising water is the least of it until it washes you away. You might be long dead before that. The hum gathers into a deep mourn for the earth's felled mother done emptying her womb for an ungrateful spawn she pushes out and spills. Sign-metal wrenches, tree-trunk fiber rips like bone and sinew, and the only missing sound is human voices—except over there, way over there, behind, off to the sides.

Drew's in my room smoking weed (I granted him permission for the duration of Stella), and I'm in Javi's, and the boat rocks. The waves are a long ways away. First it's wind and rain.

Key West Funeral

THE FUNERAL FOR Harlan Douglas, "Cherry de Vine,"
was New Orleans jazz–style. Dead Douglas, a former
high-church Episcopalian, had been cremated and his
ashes locked in a safe in the offices of St. James Church
until his bequests and last wishes could be fulfilled and his
lawyer in New York could release money from a special
account to pay for them. Douglas wanted no images of
himself displayed, not even his talent glossies, a fact that
intrigued mourners like Dan, who'd never seen him per-
form as Cherry de Vine here or in New York, Fire Island,
or Provincetown. Douglas, according to the flyer being
handed out, had graduated in chemical engineering from
Cornell and been a Marine in Vietnam before his discharge in 1972, when he'd runner-upped in the first-ever
Miss Gay America Pageant, held at the Watch Your Hat

& Coat Saloon in Nashville, losing to an Arkansas state representative performing as Norma Christie. This was according to the single-sheet program Dan got from a card table set up on the sidewalk near the AIDS Memorial at the foot of the White Street Pier. You could also take one of the Mylar balloons taped by their violet ribbon tails to the edges of the table, although the same balloons were going a lot faster from a tanned shirtless boy handing them out under a row of coconut trees that shaded a microphone and tabletop podium. Dan recognized this kid as Blair, a fishing-boat mate he'd spent fifteen long minutes kneeling in front of in the back bar of the Duval Saloon. A construction worker on the lam from Fort Myers, Blair was straight, with a cheerfully reliable weed habit. Either way, Dan decided against a balloon. Boys liked weed, and sometimes the best way to get laid was to provide weed.

Dan had not counted on attending an open-air, New Orleans–style memorial service, of course. He'd been jogging when he spotted the crowd of two dozen or so gathering at the foot of the pier, remembered noting the occasion in last week's bar rags, and decided to stop, reading the handout but hanging back so his sweat wouldn't offend anyone. He had once been fascinated by drag queens. Growing up in the South and entering a club under age, he'd been encouraged by their forthright outrageousness. The club had been owned by the mafia, he'd been told, and his first worry about trying to get past the door man (that an Italian bodybuilder would be called in to kick his ass before throwing him out) disappeared when a giant in line wearing a victory-rolled wig and a flounced satin gown grabbed Dan's hand, blinked her black moth-wing lashes, and said, "You're coming in with me, Private!"

Later he'd found out that minors never got kicked out of the Old Plantation. The owners of the OP knew they needed window dressing (at forty-five Dan couldn't believe he'd ever been considered decorative) in order to keep the regulars loyal and give the heavy drinkers and closet queens something to look at before they got cut off or lost heart making passes at the "chicken."

"Chicken" was kids, twinks like him who snuck in.

In the heavily judgmental, surprisingly uncharitable gay world of before, you were either: chicken or a chicken hawk. At the time, at least no one that Dan knew dared believe that a gay man really wanted to settle down with another homosexual his own age. A straight man his own age, maybe. The inner world of queer exile had been as presumptuous and self-loathing and full of stereotypes as the larger one they were all trying to escape. Dan missed the old slang. He well knew that if the self-loathing lingo had survived to today, he would now be considered a chicken hawk. Kids these days had no idea of the old par-lance. Good for them. He also knew that he probably had more in common with the deceased than with Jackson.

The night before, he and Jackson had argued about Dan's drinking—and it was anyone's guess who'd won.

Jackson was young, but it was hard to judge him as naive. He knew the importance of hard work. He was sweet, admirable. The twenty-four-year-old's savings outstripped Dan's five or six times. He was a cute and fetchingly self-assured youth, but he should go a little more easily on himself. Also a little easier on Dan. After their lovemaking, Dan had enjoyed two glasses of white wine. Dan had checked: the alcohol content of the California plonk he'd bought at the drugstore was under 10 percent. It was the same, practically soda-pop-grade stuff he'd had three or four glasses of while summoning his thoughts on Louise earlier that afternoon, before Jackson returned from quitting his shitty job at Fantasy House, "the best gay resort on the planet," according to the gay travel magazine where the resort advertised online. Jackson had more work elsewhere on the island, and since he lived with his mom, he wasn't going to starve. But he was keyed-up after the sex (which Dan thought was good and dirty, a pleasing new low), and after catching his breath and lying under the covers in the quiet following a thundershower, had calmly said (without turning to face Dan while he said it), "Do you need that stuff to feel normal?" *Normal?* Because what was normal? Was to be normal not to feel in a constant state of fear, cognizant of not only death but imminent penury? (And how was *penury* pronounced?) Dan had given Jackson a pass and said nothing. He realized how frightened of his own homosexuality Jackson was. And if it wasn't his sexuality he was frightened of, then he should be. Dan was lonely, profoundly lonely in this temporary place of endless summer; he'd tried not to start a fight. He'd considered telling Jackson in a complex tangle of syntax and comic periphrasis to mind his own fucking business. He'd kissed Jackson's white polished-marble shoulder smelling of talcum powder. He'd said, "You're a lot smarter than I am. Smart as you are at your age, I think you should still just enjoy your youth." And Jackson had kissed him then—God knew why. It was almost obscene, their age difference. Jackson's mouth was a little strawberry erupting with leaks of juice: vital, innocent, although *innocent* was a dangerous and potentially meaningless word. Why should the pretty mouth crave Dan's dry, cynically curved, loathing-deformed lips? The world held multiple mysteries. Somehow, Jackson cared about Dan. So frightening. Dan had then told Jackson, "I want you to start thinking about junior college again. You'll do great." Surely that got him. Before they fell asleep, Dan heard a languid, yawny, "And I know about your secret smoking."

Dan felt light today. He'd enjoyed only three cigarettes before his run. It was a drag queen's funeral, fitting. He'd gone out for a jog and was still a little drunk from last night.

Key West had its sensual rewards but could also be suddenly punitive. Wherever you went—away from childhood, away from drunk, angry, overly happy Mom and Dad, so angry, so vital, so unbearable—they were still here, making hell and heaven together.

Today there was a bright Florida haze, the air humid and breezy. Father Bill, the vicar, wore a black short-sleeved shirt and collar and dark glasses, his long, thin, white hair pulled back into a ponytail. He strolled the crowd creakily but in his usual nice mood, no doubt eager for the reception back at the vicarage, where right now Jackson in his role as caterer was helping his friend Nicole set up. The beach, just next to where the memorial service had been, looked dull, but the water out a ways still glittered a bit. The city and island of Key West could never quite disappoint, though a beachside funeral was weird.

Off to the side, a brass quartet played throaty music. They were kids from the high school, all in their uniforms, crimson trousers, stingingly radium-white jackets. Dan didn't recognize the tune, but it was fulsome. Maybe Louis Armstrong. Dan thought he could pick out an undertow of disco in the rhythm section, but without strings disco or R&B meant nothing to him. An orchestra defined a disco classic. There was a trumpet, flute, sax, and jabbing trombone, and the beat behind them was wan and not especially danceable. There was a bass drummer booming it. The snare was a clean, precise roll, a hissing—like a single long jet of steadily emitted gas—and the young ensemble filled in with their electric, Vitusian party moves. Then nearby, Father Bill took the microphone, wrestling it out of its stand, and in the muttery, hushy way his parishioners and his barmates had come to expect, said, "Good afternoon! Harlan, I think, would say you've done him proud." Then, even less intelligibly: "I'd say *yabba-yabba.*"

Most of the crowd hadn't heard the priest's words. Those who had filled the others in, and there was applause. The applause was brief and then an old woman everyone knew as well, because she was the most reliable pot source on the island, yelled brassily, "Speak up! For Christ's sake! Talk louder! Speak into the goddamn thing!"

"I'm about to speak in the words of my dear friend, Harlan 'Cherry de Vine' Douglas, who it must be said struck himself down recently in the line of duty, which is to say Cherry was about to go on and entertain us all. I for one respected Harlan's choice. I loved Harlan, or if you like, Cherry. This was my friend. I'm feeling a little emotional now. To his words . . ."

Maybe part of Father Bill's emotion was not knowing which gender to choose.

For that, Dan found Father Bill brave. How well had the priest known the man?

Was it important, the pronoun? Key West was progressive but not full of sticklers about pronouns or the niceties. Precise pronouns, even, might have gotten in the way. It was a party town, not so particular. Father Bill went on. Funerals *ought* to be entertaining, Dan thought.

The crowd was restless. The reference to Douglas's suicide was barely a reference, more of a feathery sideswipe. At bars, Dan knew Father Bill as the queer who apparently had no sex. He was never seen to be coming on to anyone, twink or otherwise. He slumped into a drink and made no fuss, no protest, no nothing. Father Bill just wanted his drink and his rest. He lived just around the corner. It was three hundred steps from the Duval Saloon to his front porch.

Father Bill rattled the pages of the prepared good-bye speech, glanced down at them, and began, quoting Harlan Douglas, without citing him, "'And in the words of my meemaw, it's shit-or-get-off-the-pot time. Meemaw, what a gal.'"

The band had suddenly quit, making it easier for the priest to be understood.

"'I have words of advice. Date a Frenchman, Spaniard, or Italian, but marry a German, if marriage is important to you. Germans like things neat and clean and don't mind pitching in. Germans are surprisingly fun, and I always wanted to be fun!'"

Father Bill looked up, gauging the crowd. He cackled mutely.

The crowd swayed. Off in the right corner of Dan's purview, the tan, bare-chested, ephebe Blair snickered, his eyes vacant, mouth staying open.

"'So to speak, I married a German, and that was good

until I made an error of taste. But I won't bore you. The most important thing is sex. Without that chemistry, everything dries up.'"

Cheers from the crowd. Dan sort of tittered his own appreciation.

"'Love everyone. Be ready to. Anyone in the world can surprise you. Love is beautiful. It holds the world together. I never hated anyone, even in Nam. I hated my superior officers, but that was because they didn't get it. But the other guys? Gold. Treat everyone like gold. I was a stupid grunt crawling in the mud and still I knew to love. That's why I wanted out. I got out and I missed my buddies, who were gold. I have no wisdom. There's no wisdom. I almost died two or three times. I lost count. But when they flew me home? I was never the same . . .'"

Next to Dan, a man in a silver-lamé jumpsuit sipped bottled water. He seemed bored but not disengaged. He might have known the deceased, or known of him. The city and island of Key West was tight, but that didn't mean it was all a big family, no. People, particularly older ones, might put in an appearance for a festive evening, then go home as shut-ins for weeks.

"'Love like there's no tomorrow. A long time ago the late great Goldie Frisch said to me, "Bitch, go out there tonight like it's your last." She was right. Goldie was great. With her it was colorectal. "Eat roughage and get exercise. Sunshine is the best source of vitamin D on the planet. Enjoy!"'"

The band struck up a ragged, faithful "When the Saints Go Marching In" and formed a line choogling onto Atlantic Boulevard, probing the air with their joyous and dully glinting instruments against the oblivious, sheenless sky.

Owing to police regulations, they stuck to the sidewalk.

JACKSON THOUGHT SUICIDE was wrong. It wasn't much better than abortion, but still. His friends thought he was quite reactionary for a young gay man, but Jackson had his views.

He suspected that Nicole didn't care about these issues. Catholics: they were so jaded. He was putting out the crudités. The bar was set up. Why drink to the dead, why eat? He didn't believe in ghosts or souls, but he suspected some of the people about to show up could. Why turn a suicide into a party? After they showed up, did they expect Harlan to make an appearance?

His religious education had been very spotty. He'd gone to church a little, as you did in Key West: a little. He didn't have a father but had been raised by three generations of women, including both grandmothers. He'd been raised femininely. These women's idea of carrying on in life was never to dispose of anyone important by blood. They had loved him, and for him life was about love. But it needed some strictness, after all.

Jackson lived at the intersection of his own personal

beliefs and crass commerce. He was supposed to turn away when he saw something that bothered or insulted him or otherwise got his goat. Key West weather was humid, which was a perfect symbol of the social life here: everyone in everyone else's hair, hair matted to your forehead and sticking unflatteringly to your crown. Jackson buzzed his hair, not to be implicated. Messy hair was slutty, suggestive hair, maybe.

And another thing. People fell apart on this island believing in the eternal party setup. Which is what made it so annoying and sticky for Jackson, working in what was charitably called "entertainment" down here. Key West was a giant whorehouse. He'd still been working in "entertainment" when he'd picked up Harlan at the airport for his appearance in drag. It was all so unseemly, but that was Jackson's job just then.

About a half-hour before Harlan Douglas's OD, Jackson had said, "Anything else?"

They were in Mr. Douglas's cabana, and Jackson knew the bar needed ice.

Harlan, nibbling a sandwich and sipping a tumbler of bourbon, had lifted his nose serenely, and said, "I want to visit the Elysian Fields. But I'll save that for another evening."

Jackson wished now that he hadn't been so snotty. Really, the man was nice. But he hadn't been looking forward to going on stage. Jackson had told the police all of this and he thought he should give it to them from his angle. The investigating officer had fretted, saying, "Did Douglas say or in any concrete way *indicate* he wasn't looking forward to going on and performing?"

"It was in his attitude," Jackson had said. "I don't know him, but when I picked him up at the airport he was in a mood I wouldn't describe as, I don't know, jolly or, I don't know, pleasant or commodious. Maybe he was trying to impress me. And I also thought he was intoxicated."

Jackson was small and looked younger than he was, so he tried to make up for it with his vocabulary.

"Let's stick to the facts. Give me more facts. What did you see or hear?"

"He slumped in his seat. He sequestered himself behind sunglasses."

"Sunglasses. And a cap or hat of any kind?"

"What? *No.* When we got to the complex here and we settled him in the cabana, he got suddenly quiet. He'd been chattering nonstop, and like I said, we didn't even know each other."

"All right, chattering." The detective scribbled. "How's your mom? It's Linda, right?"

"Really? I mean, excuse me? Really?"

"Just tell her Terry said hi. Just 'Terry' ought to do. Now, did you see him using or holding any prescription medications, or any controlled or illicit substances?"

"I think he'd already taken care of that before getting

off the plane. Nor was I too surprised when I was working across the street at the sister bar a while later and heard."

"He didn't tell you anything odd? When you say he was chattering, do you mean talking in a loose or what one might characterize as a rambling fashion, unconnected by topic?"

"Oh, there was a lot he said that was odd, just not unusual for somebody in Key West. He talked about his life and I suppose, too, what you'd call his philosophy—giving advice, whatever. He kept getting angry at the current administration, and evangelicals."

"Did he mention recent problems that had cropped up in his life? Sustained tragedies?"

"He talked about himself, is all. That is, giving his point of view. He yammered on."

Terry pulled out a card: DETECTIVE TERRENCE CARVER.

Jackson read it. It had the official seal of the city on it. In slanty letters along the bottom under his detective title it also read SPORTS AND PUBLIC ENTERTAINMENT LIAISON. An image came to Jackson, from a few years ago: his mother staggering out of a squad car in front of their house. The siren and blue light blithered and flashed, then just as suddenly went off. It was a "fun" joke. His mother fell laughing helplessly to the weedy lawn. She waved back weakly as the car pulled away and left her there. It was up to Jackson to go out and collect her. Justice had a funny, knee-slapping definition here. Not that there wasn't real crime. There was that, too.

Jackson was poker-faced, but he felt Officer Terry's look hard-fastened to him.

"Anything else you remember, any salient details—that is, any concrete, conspicuous—"

"I know what salient means. No, Terry."

"Thank you for your time."

"Uh-huh"

"Tell Linda Terry's been wondering what's up. What a fun gal, your mom, and solid," the detective had said, without a clue about what a complete dick he was.

He hadn't made use of the number. He assumed they had everything they needed to rule it a suicide. Why should they be wasting their time? Jackson knew depressed and messed-up when he saw it. Not to put too fine a point on it, but Key West was pretty yet socially crummy.

Harlan had seemed pathetic, but almost intriguingly so. Rather like his Dan.

Harlan had requested a full procession, going from the garden bar of the French Quarter complex up Duval toward the Atlantic side and swinging out past Higgs Beach, but there hadn't been enough time to clear it. The city would have to barricade every street on the way like it was Fantasy Fest or New Year's, probably making it a bigger spectacle than it deserved to be. Drying up taxpayers' dollars. The night before, Dan had said, "Do you think that's out of homophobia?"

And Jackson could get so exasperated. "No, Daniel. It's an *expediency,* nothing more."

When he heard himself say or think *Daniel*—Daniel the Biblical prophet, the angry one, who predicted great changes for the Jews, for the People of the Book—Jackson felt like crying. Dan was anything but wise. Did he love Dan? Maybe he pitied him, poor silly Dan.

The thing about being raised cursorily Protestant was all the guilt with none of the rewards. Food, for instance; beyond drink there was a whole guilt thing about food even.

A plate of sticky pasta with no sauce, and you have to eat the whole fucking thing or you can't go to bed. How he envied the seeming freedom of the four women in his house, who called themselves Christian but did exactly what they wanted without beating themselves up. No doubt the people coming to this wake probably similarly lacked a sense of culpability, and they made it look so easy. He no longer believed, but he had the aspirations still of someone with faith, with much optimism. He looked around the room. It was the "perfect" Key West room, dilapidated and "romantic." The island nauseated him generally. It was a whore with cheap bright skirts.

He looked around, trying to find satisfaction in this seedy venue, this vicarage.

Nicole found a mirror, a mirror like a huge gold-framed

painting where her portrait listed into the center of silvery clarity, and she adjusted her bow tie. She looked over the shoulder into the mirror at him. How he knew she loved him. Perhaps too much.

She smiled over her shoulder and said, "Do I look all right?"

"You look perfect, my darling," he replied, knowing he did love her buddyishly.

He was going to lose Dan. Dan was better than anyone he'd ever been with, if flawed. But he might have to lose Dan, in order to improve his own lot in life. That was the way it was said, "lot in life." No disrespect to Dan. Dan could go from boys to women and back to boys.

He turned just as Glen came clopping up the wooden steps of the creaky porch. The first guest, and you knew he just had to be first—the motherfucker. Jackson was furious. How many times had he heard Glen knock Christianity, citing Episcopalianism as the worst denomination. And here was Glen, who'd liked to suck Jackson's toes, the doof.

Jackson went over to Glen, not fussing with his uniform, feeling confident in his cinch-waisted black vest and his blindingly bleached-white shirt—the bow tie, he sensed, straightly aimed. He didn't need to diet. He had automatic discipline, consuming little of anything, and he said, stuffily, he realized, "Why are you here?" and tried not to smirk.

"This morning waking up, I realized that I love you—and

that you're mine, or should be," said Glen, tilting his face, his glasses crooked and smudged, and he shifted the long shoulder strap of his colorfully woven, humble and small Andes hip bag.

"That's interesting."

"Don't you love me?"

"It's just interesting to hear you say that."

Glen looked pretty beat-up, which was great, typically unkempt, totally uncareful.

Glen said, "Why is that interesting?"

"I don't know, it's interesting—that's all. First you not answering my messages forever, then you did and it was all lame. Whatever."

Glen contorted his face into a series of reactions.

Glen said, "I've been in bad shape, you know that. Baby. I've been a wreck."

"What about me, Glen? And how childish was running away without telling me?"

Nearby, Nicole undid the caps on a series of tonic and soda waters. She opened them slightly and let some gas escape then retightened them. Bohemians, Episcopalians, this crowd would be all hard-core liquor drinkers, Jackson supposed.

As he'd many times seen, the vicar, Father Bill, could put away the cocktails.

Glen needed to check himself (into a facility, actually) and talk to Jackson after.

Glen said, "Angel Bear, I'm in love with you!"

Nicole looked up from her barkeeping ministrations, raising one admonishing, or else approving, eyebrow. Nicole deferred too easily to males. She knew that Jackson, twenty years younger than this goofball, was prone to tender guilt and going back. How sweet!

"Whatever, dude. What the actual goddamn fuck ever," said the generally curse-averse Jackson, and started away from this wreck. He wondered about Dan, wanting Dan to be here and see him in his triumph—so Dan could remind him of this triumph and love Jackson. Because Jackson was weak, and he knew it, and was still that Protestant, that guilty and repentant.

He turned his back to Glen, who was doing something or reacting in however way and wouldn't be allowed to bother Jackson. Jackson lately had stopped wanting intimacy, but what was that? And why? Jackson was the loneliest person he knew, just wanting to be rich.

"Jackson," said Nicole, trying to look at him—but Jackson was self-delicious.

Jackson found something to do. The surfaces in this house, a pretty good example of the Queen Anne, were appallingly dusty, and he kept tearing off double sheets of paper towel to rub at the filthy places.

After her last boyfriend, Nicole had recently gone over to girls. That seemed optimal, to be a woman who wanted to be with women. Men, whatever.

More than once, Jackson had lied that penises disgusted him.

He said, "Who cleans this place? The man's a minister. Doesn't he have a maid?"

Glen hovered, saying, "Can I see you later?"

"God, no. Will you just—I'm trying to work, honey."

"Can I have a glass of wine before I go?"

"Did you know the deceased? No, you're too uptight about drag queens and stuff. You left town the day I had to chauffeur her around, and then she killed herself. How do you think I felt when that happened? It was practically on my watch, and look at you!"

"I'm a mess, true. But only because I love my honey-bear-boy."

Which, ick. Even though it may have come from a sincere place, poor pecker.

Glen studied him knowingly, a smirk trying to break through. It was disconcerting. He had a way of suddenly going cruel—not often, just every once in a while, going un-Buddhist for an instant and looking at Jackson hatefully. Next he'd be calling Jackson's anus by dirty slangs to feminize and subvert him, the pig. Jackson felt the beginnings of a woody in his black pants. How Jackson resented this allure. Glen had not washed his hair in God knew how long. Had he swum down from Stock Island?

Glen said, "Since when do you hang out with female impersonators?"

"I didn't say I did. I said I'd met him, I was his driver. Just for an afternoon."

"I saw his show once," said Glen, "at La Te Da. He was talented. It was all right."

"I never saw him, but I would have. Oh, you can stay. On the porch, until they come."

"I'm banished to the porch."

"Put that bag under a bush or something. You look homeless. Have you bathed lately?"

"You want me to go somewhere and shower?"

"It's a religious event, silly."

"It's all a social screen," said Glen, accepting a plastic cup of wine from Nicole. "It's all samsara, the cycle of material experience, the trap of living, wanting to die and be extinguished, complete. Come die with me, to life, not real death. Just sort of die, get off samsara."

Which had its appeal, although what it looked like, this idea, who knew?

"Out of respect," said Jackson, "and to get you out of my hair, please sit on the porch."

With Glen gone, Nicole said, "That was pretty firm. He looked so sad shuffling out."

"I'm not in love with him anymore."

"Sure you are. Or you're still attracted, I can tell."

"No one's ever made him grow up," Jackson muttered, then he got bored dusting.

His hormones had nothing to do with his mind. In the morning he woke hard, torture.

More guests started coming. Jackson stepped out into the street when he heard horns playing a saggy tune and a slowly thundering offstage bass drum being beaten. He stepped back up onto the porch, being sure not to look at Glen sitting there.

Sandrine, who ran the catering company, came out from the kitchen with a silver tray. On it were minuscule delicacies widely spaced. She was French but had shed most of her accent, she had been here so long. She was never going back to France, she said—not until her mother died. But after that she was taking her money, turning around and coming right back, trying to civilize Key West one pointlessly underloaded salver of tiny goat cheese and mushroom puff pastries at a time. No one knew how old she was, forty or sixty being the usual range people would speculate within, though *her* mother, she said, was eighty-two. Sandrine said she worked to live and didn't live to work, but could handle as many as three caterings a day in season, complaining the whole time. Jackson was too wise to believe in her grousing. He romanticized her, her skimpy clothes and simple manner. It added up to some kind of elegance. Sometimes he wished she'd ask him to be her business partner. Sandrine was the only one whose personal criticism and fussing after he could stomach. He loved flirting with her. He didn't know if she liked guys or girls, though from behind with her chopped brunette hair and pencil figure she looked like a teenaged boy.

"Sandrine," he said (raising his voice so Glen was sure to hear twenty steps away, so Glen would be apprised of his ambition, Jackson's will-to-be-greater), "why don't you move your catering to the French Riviera, and Nicole and I will come work for you?"

She didn't have to think about it.

"There I could not afford you."

Sandrine's mood was good. Sometimes when she dispensed sourness, it amusingly sang.

She added, "I cannot go back to France, unless it's either to Paris or Normandy, and even then . . ."

She didn't specify. She didn't seem to care to elaborate. Sandrine's great gift was indifference, a cool apathy that sounded like a playful warmth, a special *esprit*.

Jackson and Nicole both adored her thin-striped sailor blouses, so simple.

Nicole said, "But if we all went, Jackson and I could learn French."

"You would do better to stay here and use your Tagalog in useful, beneficial ways, so you could help some of your own people. Start an employment agency for Filipino émigrés."

"I don't think so," said Nicole, "and, besides, there aren't so many Filipinos around here."

"You could go somewhere else. Go to Maryland. You could make a fortune."

"Maryland?" said Nicole. "Where do you get that?"

"Once I was there, it was nice. And I love the crab, so fresh and tasty."

Sandrine, who rarely was seen snacking or doing anything with food but arranging it.

Jackson said, "Sandrine, you're the one who's always saying money isn't everything. We love that about you. Sandrine, you're the yin and the yang!"

"I meant that as an incentive. It's not good to stay forever in the place where you grew up and assumed yourself, your adult, grown-up self I mean. Does that make sense?"

"Myself," said Nicole, giggling, "my Tagalog sucks."

"I see. Well, you should learn while your mother is still alive."

"Not for much longer, she isn't."

Sandrine seemed shocked by the matter-of-fact, almost cheerful way Nicole announced this. Personal matters were not to be mentioned among colleagues.

"You're a naughty girl. Oh, they're coming. You hear all the car doors closing? Why do the Americans drive everywhere? It's a small island. Even here, there are shockingly few bikes."

"Bikes are for tourists."

"This is what I'm talking about—these attitudes. Where do they come from? If you went on a bike, Nicole, you would lose an extra ten pounds easily. And if you stayed away from rice."

"I'm happy with the fifteen I already lost. I'm always hungry for the rice I don't eat."

When Sandrine had placed the platter of puff pastry on the long cloth-covered table, and gone back to the kitchen, Nicole said, "Have you noticed, she doesn't like being contradicted?"

Jackson said, "It's cultural, I think. Just tell her you already have one mother."

"Yeah, but not for much longer."

She said it distractedly. Nicole lived to work, to stay away from home.

SHE'D LEFT ZACH at home with his brushes and paints. He was starting to get deadline-frantic. His gallery showing was two weeks away. He carped that he probably wouldn't sell anything, anyway.

Once when she'd said something awful to him about someone she knew he loved dearly, he'd drawn her a Venn diagram of their relationship. She was a triangle and he was a blob, or an imperfect oval. Where they overlapped, one of the corners of the triangle pierced him just where the oval was slightly crimped. He had done it on a scrap of heavy sketch paper with a brush and black paint, just the two shapes, and posted it on the fridge without labeling or giving it a title; he didn't have to, it was obvious whose pointy corner was going into the soft, vulnerable blob. That night, she'd refused to cook. They'd gone out for crab cakes instead. When he offered to order a bottle of her favorite Chablis, she'd said, "Nope, not tonight, I don't believe." She'd dared him to default to his usual glass of scotch and ice, silently, with a proud stare. The next morning they'd fucked harder than usual. Funny how these things turned around overnight. After the restaurant, she'd gone home to bed and he'd sat up drinking scotch, maybe moving to his studio to look at sketches and studies, then waking with the hangover hots. Like it or not, Zach was always the one in control—when she wasn't the one in control. Jane loved Zach.

Now she thought about turning around before stepping onto the porch of the vicarage and walking briskly home, letting herself in quietly to read. She thought about a lot of things. But she was curious. People and their talk were her subject.

Jane was a writer, after all, and the observations and ideas that drove her writing kept her head in a state of constant agitation. In the past she'd done volunteer work for Father Bill during periods of creative fallow, and she thought now that she'd gladly paint this shabby porch, if she were a decorator (what she'd wanted to be), in any scheme the diocese deemed appropriate—a soapy lavender, psycho purple trim, hippie colors.

AHEARN, PRISCILLA JANE (1948–)

"Priscilla Ahearn" would have made her sound like a romance novelist, God help her.

She liked sneaking through the world as Jane, plain Jane, the novelist Jane Ahearn.

When she and Zach had first moved down, she'd liked Key West because it reminded her of San Francisco, if San Francisco were cleaner and had better weather. Key West was said to be part of the redneck riviera, was its out-to-sea unofficial capital, but she found it far more tolerant than their old neighborhood in New York, where the original ethnic families and poor artsy types had been chased out by yuppies. Young working couples with fertility-drug twins pushed around in double-wide strollers by tired West Indian nannies—puzzled-looking kids who were sometimes old enough to walk. Even the gay men (who Jane would have thought had fled the heartland to escape family) were getting in on the act, adopting orphans of wars or floods and earthquakes, or hired down-on-their-luck girls to smuggle their sperm into, before the babies came out of them and they were gotten rid of. She'd known Zach was for her not because Zach was self-sufficient, which thank God he was, but because the last thing he wanted was a child to compete with his other creations. They shared a distaste for squalling brats—or maybe they were not brats, they were perfectly intelligent, imaginative youngsters who might very well grow up to become reasonable, productive citizens. But who the hell had the time to find out? One of the original hippies but now a "literary voice," she didn't regret not having children, Jane's students were her children, meaning they could be lazy with low attention spans. Her parents, were they still alive, could hardly have understood.

Her main literary subject was spoiled adults, whom she liked to catch acting like children. And she considered herself spoiled (see above stream-of-consciousness). Her mother had hoped for a grandchild. Before going howling into the night (quite literally, the nurse had attested), her mother during her most lucid moments would say, "You were always a grownup, even as a little girl, but a terrible, terrible sensualist. You crushed cut flowers to your face. Slurped your soup."

She and Zach came every year for the sunshine and bougainvillea, but it did seem like her allergies, along with the mosquitoes, were getting steadily worse.

The good novelists didn't fit squarely into any place, but here she could get work done. She'd sort of stumbled into her career but made it through extremely hard work, yet she was also lucky. She was one of the good novelists, she'd been told.

She'd been sixteen when she went to her first protest, but as an older boy had pointed out, she'd looked about twelve. She'd looked around at the others in their sandals and jeans; she was the only one there in heels. Yet everyone had been nice. Her father was disappointed in her, and her mother embarrassed by her. The other night she and Zach had watched a documentary about the folk music festival in Newport, something in black and white that at the time was considered the last word on the power to change the world by singing in a syrupy quaver. She and Zach had not known each other at the time, but he'd been doing similar things in other parts of the country. He'd gone to Alabama and Mississippi, gotten busted, and spent the night in jail. Jane had looked over at him. The footage was truly gripping. Such attractive boys. She noticed that most of the festivalgoers shown on screen and interviewed saying loopy, abstract things were cute, clean-cut boys, any one of whom she would have gladly dated back in the day. But the stuff they were saying. At the first commercial break, Jamie Lee Curtis selling a yogurt that was supposed to make you more regular than the usual brand did, she turned to Zach and said, "Were we really that self-assured and on top of things—and so fucking self-righteous?"

Zach's messy-haired head was still in the studio, mixing pigments, and he'd said, "It's all in your books. Isn't that what your writing's all about, always has been?"

"I know," she'd said, getting up. "I was being rhetorical. But amazing, huh?"

Living the life, to what end? Maybe so they could find each other, be in love.

Zach then had nodded, sipping an iced vodka.

She'd seen Cherry de Vine at a piano bar here on Duval

caterwauling torch standards and, the best part, tearing the hecklers apart. It was too strong meat for Zach, but although she'd never met Harlan Douglas or offered her expression of arch gratitude after a Cherry de Vine show— she had never laughed so hard or felt that grateful to be alive (her writer friend Perry had gone with her for her first show)—she'd gone back each night all through Cherry's engagement, and felt this affinity.

"Can you, can you," she heard across the crowded front room of the vicarage, as though a postmodern confessional poem was being steadily recited, "could you possibly gimme a dollar?"

In the background she heard Grand Funk, an old fave, overlaid with a rap refrain:

We gonna whip yo booty!

The rap fit the beat, odd variation of "We're an American Band," a funky update.

VILDA WAS A go-go dancer, inscrutable and straight. He was tall, tightly muscular, and golden, his skin almost the same shade as his hair, his nose like a smooth, perfect hacking instrument, curved and mean. His whole body looked like it would prefer to be naked—and, of course, he hadn't finished putting his uniform on. He was still attaching his bow tie. His polyester vest was unbuttoned, while the house was already half full, and he stood in the middle of the party getting himself together. Cherry de Vine, from beyond the grave, had requested they call this a party; Cherry de Vine had requested, especially, Vilda's presence.

Adjusting his tie ineffectively, Vilda scooted up beside Nicole, late as usual, laughing, saying, "Hey, how are you guys doing?"

His idiomatic English was always a tad off. He said further, "Having a good time, you guys?" and grinned foolishly, yet how could you resist that naturally straight smile?

To Jackson he sounded like a beach-bum vampire, unaware of the night-feeding sharks as he surfed through life. You never saw him at noon, but you always heard him coming, his loudly adenoidal voice making light about something he might not have even understood as it was being said. He laughed about nothing and regularly got on Jackson's nerves, getting on them now by nudging Nicole aside behind the bar and saying, "I'm here, so I can take over. Sorry I've been late . . ."

Nicole shifted demurely over next to him, her high, flat cheeks flushing.

Jackson hissed into her ear, "Are you going to let him do that *again*?"

Jackson loathed the Czech's habitually airy tardiness, but Nicole he knew was smitten.

Vilda had already fixed his stare into the crowd, foolishly saying to Jackson, "What?"

Jackson fisted his hand on his hip. "Nicole set this whole fucking bar up, and now *you*?"

"I don't understand."

"You come late, don't do any of the setup, you expect to collect the same amount as—"

"I don't have to make the same amount. Take more than me. Money, who cares?"

"All right, we'll see about that with Sandrine."

"I am fine," said Vilda. "You should maybe pull your head out from your ass."

"Is that a gay thing; a cute little wry, sly slur? About my head and my ass being gay?"

"It was anything you imagine. It was nothing. I don't care, I do my job."

"Interesting," said Jackson, looking at no one. "He thinks he's doing his job! *Wow.*"

Vilda said to Nicole, "Your friend likes talking to himself very much. Wow."

Nicole snickered and headed for the kitchen, picking up an empty tray on her way.

Vilda, knowing the object of his income, eyed the room for the priest, one of his best tippers. Jackson knew about that. There was never groping, though the old guy did like to have Vilda bend as he stashed the bills in his G-string right along the hip. This town, these stragglers.

Jackson found Dan, hugging him and saying weirdly, "I'm sorry, but Glen's here."

"Was that him on the porch?"

Dan smelled freshly showered and was dressed in a jacket, shirt, and jeans, no tie.

"How did you know?"

"He just looked so lonely."

"I think the woman behind you knows you."

Dan smiled queasily. It was Jane. He hadn't seen her since some time before Louise had died. Once Jane and Louise had been friends. He didn't know where he and Jane stood now. As survivors, why shouldn't they speak? All around them, death. But what was left for the living?

"I've been meaning to write you a condolence," said Jane. "Are you all right?"

"Okay. Obviously, I haven't had enough time to process. It's been four months."

"I heard the day it happened. I was on book tour. I wanted to call. Funny how we just can't always get around to doing what we know are the most important things."

They both wondered if they should hug, but the right moment might have already passed.

"I hated Louise's stupid tiff with you. I never got it," he lied. "And I never had a chance to get your side of it. I didn't know if I should call or write."

"Probably for the best," Jane said, then offered Jackson her hand and said, "Hi, I'm Jane."

"I know who you are, you're a writer here. We did that benefit, where you talked?"

Dan said, "This is Jackson Stone, a native. A Conch!"

"Oh, a native," she said, smiling. "Well about that night, I probably made no sense whatsoever. But how can anyone, talking about Americans and our relations with Haiti?"

Jackson said, "I heard the donations overall were pretty generous."

"White upper-middle-class guilt," she said and laughed.

"Maybe," said Jackson. "Anyway, back to work."

Jane said, "Good luck with this crowd, right?"

"I can handle them," he said, suddenly sophisticated to Dan, socially adept.

"Nice to meet you."

"Nice to meet you."

"A friend of yours?" she said.

"I'm not always sure."

"Are you ready for guys again?"

"Oh, sure. It's not that."

"Lucky you. You can choose from both sexes. Forgive me for butting in where I have no business, but maybe it's time. They say it takes a year, but I think there are shortcuts."

The Czech dude Dan knew from the Odyssey came with a tray of different drinks.

"How are you guys doing?" he said, flashing that wallet-loosening smile.

"Just mineral water," said Jane. "I'll never make it home otherwise."

"Who said you should even go home?" said the Czech. "There are other things to do."

"Did he just say that?"

"I think he did," said Dan, who took another white wine. "You just had a moment."

"I'm lucky I know which side my bread's buttered on."

"I didn't until I met Louise," he said.

"Awh!" She reached over and patted his hand. "Sweet pudding, you'll be all right."

"I miss her. I'm not sure why I'm telling you this, but there were times when I got so annoyed by her, her fussiness, her controlling, her neediness and bossiness. I was thinking maybe it wouldn't be such a bad thing when she's gone. That it would be a relief."

He cringed theatrically, but there was a clutch in his voice at the end.

"I don't see anything wrong with saying you thought that. Sounds perfectly human."

"Thank you. It hasn't been that much of a relief. But I can think again. And I look at someone beautiful and want to cry, I'm so grateful they're there, maybe for me."

She gave surprised eyes, as though to say: *Bit too much information?*

But then she nodded serenely. Socially, Jane could careen about with her gestures.

"So, were you at the pier before? Was it a scream? I was late coming from something."

It was either the wine or the topic, but Dan didn't have any idea what she'd just said. Or he searched his mind and found it, but just. He was thinking about Jane and Louise, about the tiny kingdom of literature in America—where no one read anymore anyway.

YOUNG, HE'D STRUGGLED with alcohol, then drugs, and then a combination—going solely back to drink again as he entered middle age, when he'd begun reading and understanding from the Fifth Precept that intoxication was the only thing holding him back from becoming a bodhisattva. An up martini with olives, this was his cross, so to speak. The Buddha had obviously taught that life was struggle, and that the only way for it not to be a struggle was to surrender to struggle. It had taken him eight days sitting under the *pipal,* his beloved bodhi, to figure that out. It was all myth or allegory, but you couldn't find a better or more realistic teaching. The problem was desire, the most human of problems. The Buddha, quite the character, from what Glen had studied, anyway, just before he died had told his followers: "Strive on." Like thanks, Gautama Buddha! He was a joker somewhat, and a vegetarian, but ironically may have eaten bad pork merely to be polite. A desire to please others, not be rude, had gotten the fatal best of old Siddhartha. Glen didn't give full release, not even when they asked. He'd already said so in his ad and on his card: SORRY, NO "HAPPY ENDINGS." That most tragic and Western and common of self-delusions. They'd ask and he'd just laugh corporeally. Nothing much else to say about that, except that Christ had had less of a sense of humor, apparently. Else his disciples were more gullible, taking the Messiah at his word when he'd led them to believe he was coming back—and soon. Still waiting! *Salut, Jesu.* Or, that other thing. Where he supposedly had foresight, but if he'd seen what was coming and told the others what to expect, even guessing Peter's denial of him, why did he act so surprised up there, crying out? Dramatically, the Passion had to work two different ways to work at all.

You read the gospels of his youth, the whole Bible in fact, with 3-D glasses.

The problem for everybody in the spiritual realm was fucking; the other was not fucking.

Glen was getting tired of the massage racket. His seams were loosening; he was coming apart just as promised. He had to keep telling himself about the inevitability of struggle. He did yoga, meditated. He read enlightened texts, all of it, but it didn't mean he couldn't have fun. He felt playful, the old mischief creeping in. He *enjoyed* alcohol. He *longed* still for Jackson.

Lightning flashed, not so nearby. The sky had been darkening. The wind had picked up. And when it flashed, Glen counted two or three seconds before he heard thunder. The rain hadn't begun falling, but you smelled ozone. It was rich in the air. Across the street he saw the red soft-top antique Corvette with its top down. He stirred in the wicker chair on the porch and got up.

He was thinking about the time in his uncle's Corvette—his sexually abusive uncle whom he'd loved—riding to Memphis. They were riding away from the Ozarks and that tacky Passion Play, everything tacky in his life. And what a beautiful machine, such worldly attachments! He was hallucinating. He'd drunk a bottle of tequila before arriving. He was in love, still so in love.

He went inside, yelling, "Whose Corvette is that? Whose Corvette with the top down?"

The hot bartender, whatzisname, hollered, "What's going on? Does it rain now? Crep!"

Father Bill, tilting a cocktail to his lips, said, "Who wants to see my banyan tree?"

Several people in the room, including Glen himself, said, "I do. You have a banyan?"

This was a vicarage, for chrissake. How did they not know about the banyan of the priest they said they loved? Charity, good works! Cocktails on his porch each day! Tropical verdure was sacred to Glen, who was still in love with Jackson, and so jealous.

He remembered a summer in Europe, not this eternal, infernal summer of here—yet one where morning and evening skies were blue, and all below was green. There were cherries and apricots, such fruit. The light at the extremes was blue yet during the day so mellow and golden.

He was running from the Ozarks and the Passion Play in Eureka Springs, where he'd first tasted herb. He preferred to call it herb. And then he was running with his horny uncle. But the past, all of it (though better), was completely gone. The future was pale. You died, being reborn, your choice how, if that made sense, which he believed just did, if you looked at it correctly.

Among his other failings, he was claustrophobic. He went up the cramped stairs.

Someone said, "I hope no one farts!"

Then Glen was up there with them all, a small crowd. The covered deck was packed. The tree was magnificent. You felt like leaving this town, then you'd have this view. Saw magical things. Considered suicide, then changed your mind. Remembered the boy, the smell of him, his feet, his hair, his ears.

A HOMELESS MAN was here. People made room for him, owing to his odor. He was wearing a peach Izod with a broad diagonal bleach stain down the front, plaid Bermudas, and a pair of leather flip-flops. He'd shaved cleanly for the occasion, yet his cheeks and neck were nicked and in places gashed and flayed from the razor. A scrap of toilet paper with a dull lozenge of blood at its center patched a spot over his Adam's apple. He held his clear plastic cup of white wine delicately from the bottom, rotating it at eye level as though to inspect the color and clarity.

Who had let this guy in? People looked around at one another, aghast. Cheerfully so.

Dan and Jane stood near the open front door and Dan heard the man say, "Cherry was my buddy. He used to come out and visit me in the mangroves and suck me off. I let him, for free."

Jane said, "I'm not proud of the way I reacted. I always loved Louise. It's just that—"

"I know," said Dan, thinking, *I'm getting loaded.* "Like I said, not the easiest—"

"But everyone knew you loved her. I think only here could people understand that."

A gay man, worshipping a woman, but such a talented woman. A fiercely independent woman. He wasn't bi. He'd just loved Louise. Now he had the opinions of others to deal with.

Jane said, "Actually, I had lunch with Lily today. That's why I didn't make it in time for the memorial. I hope you don't think it was inappropriate, but I asked about you. Lily acted like she wasn't sure, but she'd look across the deck at the little cottage and everything seemed hunky-dory to her. Says, though, she still hasn't caught sight of you. Personally, I'm glad you're here."

"Lily never got me."

"You can't go through life like that, worrying about other people's opinions. Who cares? People wonder about Zach and me. We just knew. Louise knew. You knew. Screw the others."

Dan thought about his life. He'd loved a woman. He, a homosexual man, who never before would have been able to believe he could love a woman—he'd loved one who'd just died. And he was going to go home and have more to drink, for another thing.

He said, "And now I'm alone, which is odd too. Being here's half-paradise, half-torture."

Jane said, "Did you know, Louise's the reason I'm here, and that Zach and I are here?"

"I can't imagine what it was like for you guys, the original crew, back in the old days."

"It wasn't that great. There were laughs, but you were always looking over your shoulder."

"You guys just drifted apart. Then had some kind of argument?"

She looked quickly away, then looked back at him.

"Dan," she said, "in your opinion, was Louise depressed a lot?"

He wondered if like Jane he should have taken mineral water from the Czech, whose name he remembered was Vilda. He could always drink back at Lily's guest cottage. Louise had loved it there. They'd go back and forth between her little house on Pine and the cottage he rented from Lily.

He said, "Louise went through periods."

"Wet and dry, you mean. When I met her, her only poison was Orange Nehi."

"Periods where she didn't touch the stuff, not one drop. Weeks. Months, for a while," said Dan, as he was losing the thread, and watched her pause—in horror, maybe.

"Who am I?" said Jane. "Look at me. I don't drink a lot, but I drink a little every day."

The homeless man laughed fruitily at a remark a woman wrapped in bands and layers of tulle and velour was making. Seeing that a line had formed at the bar where the hot Czech go-go boy had left it to go raise the top on his car, Nicole hurried over with a tray of crudités arranged on a bed of coarse sea salt, its dip contained on the side in a ramekin like an above-ground pool in an oasis. The homeless man said, "Oh," and Nicole stopped. He reached for a radish and dunked it and Nicole smiled awkwardly. Already the colorfully dressed woman who'd made him laugh moved out of his zone, but he didn't notice. Nicole turned and the homeless man made little kissing sounds, and she hurried away.

A large black dog came out of the driving rain, bounding up the porch steps. It paused on the porch and shook its coat violently, three good hard times, then stepped

192 · MICHAEL CARROLL

confidently across the threshold, then toed more tentatively into the crowd. He was a mutt, with all the spirit
mutts had, the kind of dog Louise had liked—Louise, the
New England pure-breed. He was less an omen than a
reminder. She'd gone the way her father had. Jane heard
that it had started with a pain in her side, hard and throb-
bing and radiating to the back. She'd excused it with Dan to
drinking too much liquor; she would go back on the white
wine. White wine, a post-sixties panacea. But that was all
Jane had heard, though she wanted to hear more from
Dan. The black dog a sufficient diversion, Jane and Dan
walked away from each other, neither knowing whether or
not they'd ever talk to each other or see each other again.
That was middle age, the sudden, slow good-bye.

HALFWAY ACROSS TOWN, Zach Hooper listened to Fats
Domino, "Kansas City." It bomped and carried him bump-
tiously forward as he mixed titanium white, cadmium
orange, and Naples yellow, leaving out the ultramarine as
the foot was the one feature of the girl not in the shade. It
was a local scene, lovers picking up their things around the
pool. In the scene—he hoped you could tell—they were
about to go in for a cocktail mixed by the tiny dark figure
of a man who was mostly a violet wraith nowhere near the
dappling of the late-afternoon honey sun. The scene was
closed in by green and blue and black, the tropical foli-
age that framed everything. Fuchsia pops of bougainvillea

blossoms. But the foot. It stepped out. Zach waited for Jane to return, but pray tell not before he'd palette-knifed his creation on and smoothed it into a narrow, if not quite detailed, flesh-loaf of sweetly extended femininity. An impression of her pretty foot, which he'd lived with happily forever, his lover's. Glanced at out of the corner of your eye, just as you were recalling something, or someone, else. The color, the chiaroscuro. Mellow glints of gold light.

Earthly materials, earthly living, and somewhere beyond that a vision: maybe a knowing, but dimly, of spirits. The far world of spirits, the purified nothingness of us.

Every Night, a Splendor

THIS BARTENDER WAS a braggart, a wag, an entertainer who vamped about behind his bar, all but openly declaring himself shameless as he called out his rapidly dispensed stories of *amour,* his playlist pumping all around us. Youngish, still slender, Davy wore a Yankees cap, and no one on any night worried about how much hair there was or wasn't under the cap. He did the nine p.m. to four in the morning for a mixed crowd, and often there were young straight women on hand. Quite unexpectedly from behind the bar, Davy would pause, always opportunely, and lean back against the spottily lit counter behind him, then lower his jockstrap: the jockstrap, the cap, a sleeveless tee, tall soccer socks, and white sneakers were all he wore. Only if you were at the right end of the bar and leaning up over your drink could you see it. The flesh just above his flat pubic bone was pierced horizontally by an inch-long silver bar, a silver bead at either end of it glinting, the presumably blond pubic curls—Davy's eyebrows were water-pale—having been shaved and regrown to bright nubs. He removed and plumped his wang, he kneaded it, pulled on his also-bare scrotum and rattled his nuts by shaking his hips. He let the jockstrap snap back into place, hopped away from the counter, dancing rather like a jolly cast member at a Disney park, and then returned to serving his newcomers and regulars, fluidly, cutely, and archly. Wavy Davy.

"I said I'll serve it any way you like for five C-notes, and that's just what I did!" he said, then, "What the fuck can I get you, baby? Gentlemen, how are you? How're y'all tonight?"

It was a dirty theme park, where guys sometimes had sex, or did foreplay, or simply got naked. You could surrender your clothes, all of them, which Davy stored under the counter in a grocery bag with your name Magic-Markered on it. This was Hornyland, Ass World, Dick City.

A braless girl would take off her top and swing it to the music, jiggling those titties.

Once a thin duffer in a trilby, smoking (legal indoors here), wheezed and mimed hilarity off to the side, then rose to scream foolishly and self-deliciously: "Shootchoo dead, hunny!"

Davy sloshed ranks of shots for all around, dancing, and scooped up piles of loose bills.

The right house, the smack beats, the instantly poured booze, smokes, innuendo, fucks.

Down here everyone was dying, each at a different speed. There was a romance to all the dying, a moody, briefly sheltered romance out of Stevenson, out of early Defoe, Genet, old pirate movies, Hollywood, fading family sea prints from childhoods nearly forgotten—all in a back bar hidden just off Duval Street. Everyone a cast member in the Lost Boys theme park.

"Last call, ladies and gentlemen, I regret to inform you, last call! Drink up, final orders?"

CATTY-CORNER WAS the French Quarter House—maybe more abject in its ambient decadence and prouder in its general shamelessness, an all-male guesthouse, its garden bar never closing. It had a hot tub and pool. Within its walls the few runaway-type boys sort of relaxed among bears and their cubs, and the old men, too. Shots all around happened, two-for-one pours. Loud house music. It was Key West resembling itself, yet this year the weather was spotty. Guys wore their fleece, except for the cute boys not quite shivering in their nakedness. The palms and exotic out-of-place tropical vines with shriveling blossoms might temporarily be shrinking from nor'easter winds. And the sky no one looked up at raced with fleets of ragged clouds, dragging the moon's light in smears left-to-right above hunched shoulders. The night is long but life is short, that sky was saying. Drink up, have sex—you know you want it. Float the idea of cash if you must. You know you want it, you know you took out enough from the ATM. You know you believe in love, or its approximate, silvery cloud–fleeting equivalent. Tonight, she's almost through, as night has its feminine principle to be finessed. And there will always be tomorrow, but life just looks long.

A COUPLE BLOCKS away my wife, Deirdre, and I were sitting talking at the Monkey Bar, and she touched her clavicle saying, "I'm just not comfortable with this music. It's so aggressive, so—"

I waited a time. Like us, the guy onstage was drunk, doing his karaoke Guns N' Roses.

You can smoke in Key West bars and she sipped sloppily at her cigarette.

"So male?" I said.

"For lack of a better word."

I waited till she looked around at me, and I said, "Well, you loved it in high school."

"I did not, Gary."

"You loved it when Josh McIntyre said he loved it."

"I was a different person then. You're right, I did a little."

"That's not what you said at the time, when you were in love with him. You *loved* it."

"Times change. I didn't know then. I didn't know about myself. You know that, Gary."

"Just say it, you were in love with Josh McIntyre. We've been through this before."

"Why are you quizzing me?"

"You're just being a little difficult, a little hypocritical, kind of crazy. And drunk."

"Oh," she said, turning and getting me in her sights, "like your mother?"

"You're such a mean person. You know what you are, a mean little girl."

"Now you're turning me on. Why, you're making me want to talk to this guy when he stops singing and gets offstage. Is that what you want? You know me, I'll talk to his ass."

"I know it, baby," I said and laughed. "I know you will."

She was Dennis then, a left fielder with long legs. We met in study hall. Fairmount was where James Dean came from, and where we all met as kids. Dennis reminded me of him. Now Deirdre lives up in Miami where nobody notices. Deirdre and I have gone way-legit.

It was last call. The guy was doing the last karaoke, his and our swan song, "November Rain." How I love her and how I need her, but something about the town, which we occasionally visit when we need to blow off steam, makes me want more, though again I love her, know she's the one for me, the way he'd been the one for me. The town makes you yearn for adventure, and Deirdre wants to be—at her leisure—Debbie Reynolds, Connie Francis, a diva of our parents, the idea that Hollywood suggested to the country. A singing housewife, with this addition: Deirdre is the number-two Realtor of Coral Estates hoping to become number one. No one suspects except online that we're not the usual churchgoing, straitlaced, Trump-voting Christian couple. (I do suspect, however, that Deirdre helped vote his ass in. For weeks we avoided the topic. Then she began sighing and defending him like it was reluctantly. I disposed of my horniness between her legs and up her ass, and went online for some guy to shoot up into mine or blow me in parking lots. And, full disclosure, I wasn't always safe. My last test said I'm negative. Key West is skanky.)

I LEFT PERRY—who doesn't drink or smoke and whose mobility is an issue—home at the rental. I'd chosen the back bar of the Duval Saloon where it's dark and they play porn and for the most part I can be alone with my thoughts. When I'm not, I can be merely annoyed or amused. The video monitors all around show dull filth. The pool boy suddenly accosted by the gardener: no sound, just expressions: *Oh, were you cleaning the pool? I'm cleaning the pool, I'm the pool boy hot and lithe the way you'd expect. I sure would like to inspect your drain.* They have sex on the diving board. Or that old confession-booth trope where the priest grills the young parishioner on his catalogue of recent sins. Impure thoughts. And then, inexplicably, they're in the vestiary. So corny, but I guess effective. Why else would they keep showing this crap? I need dirtier stuff.

The town is full of strangers with their stories, all horny mostly. Key West is sexy-ish.

GOD WHAT SHE wouldn't give. Guys are awful but straightforward. She isn't built for them. But what if she'd been made a guy? Guys still rule the roost, doesn't matter if they're straight or gay.

Ryan was the guy she'd want if she were male. Ryan's complete trash but loyal. She has no doubt he adored her. Once when she was sick from a stomach virus, he took time off from his job at the Radisson and he moved in for two days, cleaning up the toilet bowl revolting with her puke. He didn't just open cans of soup, he made broth, reduced chicken parts to a broth then put in vegetables he hand-shredded. He wiped her mouth with a warm, wet washcloth. Told her his stories. He said, "There was that one time, I don't know if I ever told you this. I probably did, I was probably just drunk telling you and forgot it. A guy on Grindr wanted me to come over, he'd leave the door ajar and be on the bed nude on his stomach in the next room. I got there, but then I couldn't go through with it, though I was stimulated some. It was just so ridiculous that he'd left handcuffs on the bed next to him. And the place was so filthy. Like, normally I'd be turned on?"

"Ryan."

"Yeah, baby."

"You don't have to censor for me."

"I'm not censoring. True story."

"Were you drunk at the time?"

"I was way drunk, darling."

"Mystery solved."

"Mystery solved."

She remembered the two of them laughing and looking at each other for a long time, and how sleepy she'd felt—how reassured by the slutty friend who had helped make her feel better.

It was as though his sluttiness, a true part of him, were kept on hold while he loved her.

Loved her. She was pretty sure about that part. And looked down at her like a true lover.

He'd held her all night, and when she woke up the next morning he was still holding her.

Ryan had since moved back to Detroit. But that was the thing here. People still left you.

Key West was the long broad days and the wide endless nights, nights that like the days and weeks always ended but seemed to be spreading out with enough alcohol. People left you, was the thing. Caitlin, get used to it. There was no paradise, just the semblance of paradise but that seeming—that semblance—it was everything, enough to carry you through to the next thing.

Long night with enough alcohol could become the next

night, evenings of abhorring the next day of work at the reception desk, the hostess stand, with dreams to leave all this forever.

Key West was a tease. Or maybe that was her own problem. Still looking for a Daddy.

"WINGMAN": STRAIGHT Derek's phrase for his gay buddy Rich, who was in love with Derek.

They went out together maybe once a week. Derek would go upstairs with Rich to the drag bar and they'd take in a show. Actually, there was nothing sexier than a straight man who'd go outside his normal heterosexual brain and take in a drag show. And Derek trusted Rich, who he somehow knew would never make a move on him. They sat drinking and watching the Cher.

There was no tragedy. Rich could love Derek from afar, meaning from a stool apart.

There was always a moment. Girls loved the gay world and drag, and girls showed up.

"Uh-oh," said Derek in the middle of the Cher's "If I Could Turn Back Time."

"What?"

Derek was quick seeing Gabi's dark head coming up the stairs. He was sandy-haired, and Rich thought Gabi and Derek would make a beautiful couple, or already did whenever they were getting along and back sleeping together. Rich would almost assent to watching Derek and Gabi make love. But Rich thought of himself as a sick fuck, or alternately didn't. Why should he feel bad about wanting to watch two people he liked? Okay, it was weird. He'd grown up in a small town up in northern Florida, and there the thrills were spare. Still, he meant no harm. He loved both these people, and they both talked about sex openly, and joked, and wanted to be really hip.

But on the other hand, now sex was suspect. Any desire made known could be seen as harassment. And he got that. But something was being lost? Or it wasn't. He couldn't tell—because he'd grown up hard-shell Baptist, the horniest people alive from his experience.

But Gabi and Derek were different, right? All he knew was to play along. There were "games" that lovers played out in the open. Gabi played hers now, flirty but unassuming.

She approached them and did a double take, making sure that both Rich and Derek were watching, then with her cigarette-hoarse voice said loudly enough to be heard over the recorded electronica and wobble ("I'd find a way to say . . ." with the beat swallowing every third word): "What are you two love birds up to? Here again, all alone together? What am I missing?"

Rich sort of disliked her, as she took her place between them—as expected, as always.

She was music and chance, the whole principle, why he'd been alive, because his mother had decided Rich should be alive. She was chaos, also truth. But Derek needed a woman. Just not this woman, and the threesome was something of a travesty, but it might lead to something.

Then Derek and Gabi embraced, kissing each other on the cheek, then looked at Rich and smiled, not as though to ask *What?* but to say hello. *Hello and look at us. Aren't we fine, the two of us, but also the three of us too?*

They're going to leave me. He thought this, drinking it away.

That couldn't happen. They've broken up too many times, exchanging too much ill will.

It worked like this (he was just finishing and reordering his vodka and could hang on to a shred of the thought): they were a team, a molecule of three atoms bound by mysterious charges of affinity. It meant they were all emotionally involved without needing to explain these charges.

Or not quite. Or just not wanting to, not wanting to spoil the fun, the drama. Hence drag.

The Cher got done and Gabi turned and asked him, "So what are you working on, babe?"

"A long rambling thing I call a personal essay because I don't know what else to call it."

"Stop!"

"Leave the man alone," said Derek, paying for the next round.

"Is it a novel and you're just embarrassed to say? Because your novels never pan out?"

Derek leaned around Gabi, who couldn't see him, and Derek frowned at Rich.

Rich said, "I don't know what I'm doing. I think I'm just afraid, or I'm just lonely."

She looked at him meaningfully and he agreed with a little nod, arching an eyebrow.

"Is she doing it?" said Derek. "Is she giving you the look?"

She turned and said, "We're trying to have a conversation, a real live conversation!"

"Don't pick on the guy, he just told you," said Derek. "Don't pick on him!"

"No, it's fine," he said, thinking that he was lonely but, thank God, not totally alone.

Gabi and Derek were in their twenties, still aiming for something, Derek day-jobbing at a water sports outfit while starting a wedding and events photography business at the same time that he was doing his artier stuff with his Holga camera, creating interesting, often moody and depressing effects in ill-lit and bohemian rooms where people their age lived and had their late-night parties. Gabi was already in *The Paris Review,* and her agent was trying to get her into *The New Yorker.* When that happened she would probably leave Key West, and what would Derek do? Rich was in his early thirties, still pitching about, still trying to forge meaning from his—it had to be said—mostly perplexing sex life. Rich had never considered suicide, but the idea of it frequently shoved him into a corner of despair for lack of other ideas (he owed twenty thousand to creditors and was still youngish, though not like *them*). But being in his thirties gave him this deceptive coolness, which is what he believed attracted younger friends. Life now was *youth*.

Gabi: "Please, Derek, I'm trying to have a conversation with Rich, a serious one."

But she laughed deliciously, perhaps delectating in the chance of another sex encounter.

And who could blame her? No, Rich had been exaggerating about his loneliness. He felt like a failure was all. And who in his thirties without means of significant support wouldn't?

He wanted to crawl into a dark, temperature-neutral space and have no friends. Wanted to believe his fate wasn't his own, that it was only a voice inside himself saying dark, mean stuff.

"Gabi, you come in here when you know perfectly well it's a guy's night out and pretend to run into us. That's just not cool. Now I invited you earlier, both Rich and I did. You said no."

"You mean sausage party. I came to break up—no, be in on—your little sausage party. I know, it's the girl, the woman, who's always the last to know. To see, because I do see!"

"Stop," said Rich, the sharpest he'd ever been with Gabi.

She was drunk, just as they were.

"We're in a drag club," said Derek. "That hardly counts as the venue for a sausage—"

Gabi exclaimed wildly: "I changed my mind! God, can a person change her mind?"

Derek hunched into his fresh drink, looking abashed and irritated simultaneously.

They drank quietly until the Beyoncé came on, when Rich said, "Lots of energy, her."

Gabi said, "Rich, am I ruining this for you?"

Rich never really had to answer, or contribute. This was just pure sexual aggression.

"A loaded question!" hollered Derek—who did seem genuinely irritated, but excited.

Rich said, "I think you guys should take a vacation together. Costa Rica's great."

"I've been."

"We've both been, just not together."

Gabi pouted. Derek laughed into his drink. The night was working its magic on them.

They watched and drank until Derek said he was going out for a smoke. Gabi went, too.

The night, the night, to be replaced by the clarity and further despair of the bright day.

Rich was alone and wanted them to last, but not more than he wanted to last happily, too.

He had a small room in a broken-down Victorian,

costing as much as New York. It had a hot plate and a barely adequate shower you could hardly turn around in to rub yourself down.

Drink smoke type piss and pour. Light up. Start over. But why? Night after night.

He should go see his parents up in Ocala soon, but he disliked them. Felt guilty for that.

OUTSIDE, UNDER THE tiki hut, they were watching the Annual Lipodystrophy Telethon from Las Vegas. Unaffected boys played naked in the pool, or cooled it in the hot tub, holding their drinks in one hand and phones to take their selfies in the other. It was only the older ones sitting under the tiki hut around the rectangular bar who drank their fattening beer and hard brown liquors and watched a scene from the all-male traveling *Cinderella*. Under the house, you couldn't make out Prokofiev's sweetly jagged score. But they'd done right to do the first scene with the stepmother and stepsisters, and the Cinderella was passably feminine, meaning reed-like if not pretty, though she did look Slavic. The stage went black, then on came a magisterial, spotlit Fairy Godmother.

Everyone under the tiki hooted and hollered, except the runaway who didn't play with the boys in the pool or hot tub. In Idaho, Trey had left behind foster parents who had kept him for the state check, sadists. Probably hadn't reported him missing, still collecting that fat state check.

Next to him was Bobby, retired, well-known, had his teeth and a condo, a scooter with a basket to ride out to Searstown or the Publix shopping center at the top, ugly end of the island.

"You just get into town?"

"I put my things in the bushes behind there."

"Where from?"

"Calendula, Idaho. My best friend Heather calls it Caligula. Did call it."

"Y'all not in touch?"

"Not in the last couple weeks. She's frightened for me, ha!"

"You hitchhiked, Kerouacky. Always wondered how long it took to hitchhike from up there."

"Now you know."

"A wit!"

"I'm sorry, I'm just nervous because I don't have ID."

"They don't ask, not usually."

"I'm not damaged goods. They didn't beat me. And I'm spiritual. I believe in Christ."

"You want to know a secret? So do I."

"You go to church?"

"Nope."

"I do. There wouldn't be science without it."

"There's a good church here, St. James Episcopal. No judgments, they say."

"I don't like charity. That's one thing I don't believe in."

"See, we're getting along famously. Father Bill's a neat guy, but a real drinker."

"That doesn't bother me. Everything started out as hydrogen, you know. Hydrogen was the first element! Our sun is the fourth version of itself, which is awesome."

"Does that mean it keeps building up and collapsing, building up and collapsing?"

The kid was losing him, almost. A pretty scenic reed of a boy, almost without any color.

"Yep. And you want to know what the first element was? Hydrogen, then kaboom."

"Then all the other elements."

"Not right away, not all of them, not every."

"Let me know if you want a drink. I'm the welcome wagon, not charity."

"You're the *what* and not charity?" said the kid, who was refreshing, and spiritual too.

"Heh heh."

A beautiful day. Bobby had done all his financials online that morning so he could focus on what mattered, the drinking, the chatting-up. Bobby had a two-bedroom condo in a tower out toward the airport next to the mangroves, where a dirty scourging horde of homeless made camp, and what a smell that was. The city did what it could, but the motto on the bumper stickers they handed out was ONE HUMAN FAMILY. The northern Virginia taxes had taken care of Bobby's initial chunk. The divorce took care of the rest. Cheerfully he whistled and hummed, because he had gotten out of all that, he was in Paradise. He was seventy and took his meds. Trey gleamed: he talked to others around the outdoor rectangular bar but kept winking back at Bobby.

He took that boy home, letting him drive the scooter. He whistled a tune and Trey yelled back, "Are you saying something?" He gave the kid the helmet to feel the wind through his gray hair, still respectably thick, which he secretly admired in himself. Got a kiss in the condo. He let Trey take the scooter out for a spin on his own around the island, then too late thought better of it: kid's a minor, you dope. *Delicious, you old dirty-dog danger queen. You never got dragged into jail down here, not in this bubba-system redneckocracy. Just keep a little cash on reserve. Sheila was taken care of and I've taken care of me. An adventure.* He was a libertarian. Laws couldn't puncture his fun. The kid got home and already had the lay of the land. Said, "There was a spot for me to park it and lock it on the end post of the bike rack next to your concourse." A smart kid, and he'd reward him with some Stouffer's lasagna and salad he'd whip up like the domestic queen he was. A real genuine queer Bobby, he. Oh, and that happened and the good ice cream fetched from Publix that cost seven dollars a pint with some prissy biscotti. And yes, that all happened, *Can't believe my luck. And he stayed, yes, he stayed for a while, quite a while.*

I didn't feel like such a pervert; it felt romantic.

After dessert we kissed again. I didn't try to press it because I knew I wasn't his Number One Romeo, but he let me, shivering, so sweet. I never hated myself less, though, preening and loving myself saying quietly I loved him, and no lie that. The kind exchanges, my hospitality, the law of the desert we understand so real in the excrement-smeared world—I'm getting out, I'm getting out, though Christ may never redeem me. Because I believe. He told me in his written word and in dreams that I was abject and He knew it, but it was okay. And He gave me Trey.

Undressed in the dark. Had him undress in the hall with the light on, that cock and his ass. Told him to come to the bed and I laid on it. Had him straddle my chest with its slack and tight-knit nipples, sucked his firm root and branch of cock, bade him turn and sit on my face and licked and munched on his anus, the pucker's velvety drawstrings contracting agreeably, until he complained of pleasure, and we both jacked off to completion. That was our sex mostly.

Trey stayed for months, I forget how many; never counted. At this point who's counting? A little heaven before I'm ash. There's perfection in that, everyone ending up ash. Have fun. I did have fun. I feel he did, until he had to go or wanted to go. We're all gone, then we're ash.

And then there's night, all alone. It keeps coming, but I'm home in the condo by then, but every evening, seeing the homeless fires, smelling the excrement, from my slender balcony. I sit down and tote it up. Not bad. Between six and seven thousand to keep him around—and I recall that dumb sacred thing I said to him every time: "Let me have some of that sweet smelly hole."

I had to waggle and knead it to get my dick into shape, licking between his fuzzy buns.

I swear I still taste it on my lips, the drunk unafraid voices below nothing to me then.

I WAS IN the dirty back bar watching porn way after midnight, just sitting there looking back and forth between the monitors hung all around while Davy's house music played. I had lost track of the time. I kept ordering Yuenglings and had stopped noticing the locals and others drifting in. I didn't notice, for instance, that a guy had come in and was standing leaning against the bar to my right, until he broke me away from my beer dream by saying something startlingly new.

The guy said, "Want to stick your hand up my ass?"

Not for an instant did I think I was imagining it, yet I decided to act like I'd imagined it.

Nor did I turn to look at this man who followed up, more loudly, with, "No, seriously."

"I heard you," I said.

I heard the clatter of dense belt buckle on concrete and him say, "Go ahead, stick it in."

"I'm not going to stick my hand up your butt."

"You can. I don't care."

"I'm not going to stick my hand up someone's ass in a bar—that would be weird."

"Man, it's not that kind of bar. Nobody cares. Just stick your damn hand up my ass."

"I'm not going to."

"There's nobody here."

"There are a few people, and anyway."

"Nobody that counts or cares!"

I ignored him, watching the video priest lean toward the grill of his confessional booth.

"Puritan," I then heard, followed by the jingling of a belt buckle being fastened, but I didn't turn.

Relocated to the vestiary, the priest and the altar boy were going at it up on the screen.

I was thinking of Perry, how he could be drawn into the corniest of porn scenarios, in his days when he still bothered with porn. Now he could be drawn into less of most things. He was withdrawing, and in a way I was, too. Someday, and it would be soon (soon for both of us, as we were a team), we would not be able to return here. Perry was back at the cottage, watching TV. Tonight, I had served him a chicken stew. The cottage didn't have an oven and our options were limited to stovetop dishes, and he'd sat at the little table in our friend Lily's cottage mooshing the food agreeably. His expressions had become dialed down when he ate or tried to remember what he was thinking when he'd started to say something, and I said, "What was that?" I'm saying that it was down to the wire for me here tonight, and in the next few nights when I could sneak out to the back bar not necessarily looking for sex—which I equated with intimacy. I probably wouldn't get any: I came with that surmise. I went with a thirst that washed away the direness of need that I could entertain without urgency. I was thinking this when I got punched in the back.

It was square in the meat and bony spinal ridges between my shoulder blades, a fistful of knuckles, and it was accompanied by a voice, one I thought I recognized through the beer-smear, saying, "Asshole!" I didn't turn at first, wondering if it wasn't the *Puritan!* guy returning.

"You're an asshole," and I recognized it as a younger voice, and I turned, hopeful as ever about the intimacy, the one I was about to lose, as soon as we'd held out long enough and had to admit Perry into a facility, death and sex of course being connected, but not now in the usual way since the hypothetical sex was mine and the death was another's, an impending death after a long and agonized wait, and how much of that was on me? "You big asshole," I heard again, turning.

It was Jeremy, and oh how I had a terrible crush on the boy, though he wasn't a boy at all.

He was grinning, which lit up his features like a lantern and killed me pleasingly.

I said, "It's getting harder and harder to get a drink in peace and quiet around here."

"You're such an asshole," he said and beamed, which then perplexed me. He was drunk.

Jeremy was no kid, he was in his thirties, but catch him in the light like this, see him cut a lithe silhouette, and you'd think he was a teenager, his frame described in clean-curving lines and soccer-practice proportions. A prettily bloom-of-youth Patrick Stewart, Jeremy kept his receding brown hair neatly clipped on his long, northern European skull (the "dolichocephalic" shape they called it in the nineteenth-century anthropology texts that had led to the mistake of eugenics), no second chin threatening the scythe-stroke of his jawline, and Jeremy's horn-rimmed glasses were Poindexter-perfect to the task: he ran the Little Coral Players theater—and they did musicals and serious plays, and Jeremy had been beached here after a stint in New York doing Off-Broadway. He didn't belong here, was my judgment, but then neither did I. Again, he was younger than me, but if he wasn't careful he'd be stuck here much longer than was advantageous. In the summer he went to New England and worked his magic there. To be frank, we weren't so different from each other, but Jeremy had to scramble for cash for his productions and ventures, although he never acted like it was any big deal. He wasn't from money. So many artistic types here were from money.

A good bit of the money for the Little Coral Players came from a magician of the Silicon Valley food-ordering app, Dinnernet, a man who at forty-something was already retired and here.

I think I loved best about Jeremy that he'd achieved something, too, while desiring more. Jeremy had graduated from NYU and was here doing his thing, living the dream, which was a lot more than I could say about myself. He was young and vital and I felt old and edging on useless. I couldn't finish my second book, which in any event no one was awaiting.

Jeremy was putting on Sondheim regularly, to applause.

He took the empty stool next to me. There were very few taken stools at this hour.

Jeremy ordered a beer and rebooted the social software. He sighed: "How're you, man?"

"I'm okay."

"How's Perry?"

"He's okay, too."

Jeremy leaned away and pulled out a pack of American Spirit yellows and dropped them and his lighter on the bar, and took his time dragging his voice out to say, "Just don't ask."

I said, "What's wrong, darling?"

"Don't call me darling. And don't ask."

He was in that kind of mood I'd seen him in, which normally I took as a challenge.

"I'm sorry," I said as he paid for his drink, his facial features briefly empty-looking.

He said, "Don't be an asshole. You don't know. You're an asshole and have not a clue."

"What you've been through."

"Let me finish!" he said and drank some beer and yet didn't elaborate.

I hazarded, "So where've you been tonight?"

"None of your business," he said with a joyous finality.

"I'll mind my own business."

"You're not curious?"

"You have a difficult job."

"Not true, I love my job."

"I feel like you're about to call me an asshole."

There was always something noir about younger Jeremy, able to torque and pivot with a smooth tone and some hard, brittle words. Again, part of what I liked about him but didn't love.

He lit a cigarette and made me wonder why I was even there.

I was a Sydney Greenstreet–type character player.

As he fumbled with his cigarette, I ventured further, fruitily: "Am I an asshole, Jerms?"

"You are such a son of a bitch. My job is hard, okay? It's tricky. No, it's not tricky, it's not hard, it's just a job, a real job. It happens to be the best real job I've ever had. I'm content."

I waited. He fumbled, drank, and smoked. A near-eternity went by. I recalled the time when I tried to kiss him in the rain outside this bar and he'd punched me, saying, "No kissing!"

"It's all cool," he said, and dropped his cigarette onto the bar, and I let him pick it up.

I said, "I don't doubt it. I'm going to finish my beer and help you get into a taxi."

"No, I'm going to finish my drink, which I just ordered and which I just started to enjoy."

I said, "I get that."

Had he had a date, a disastrous or else emotionally confounding date?

"What the fuck am I doing here," he said after the next inhale, dropping the lighter.

"You tell me. You're accomplished," I said, but that didn't seem to satisfy.

"Dick."

"I'm just trying to be supportive. I loved the *Sweeney Todd*," I said.

I lied about having seen the *Sweeney Todd,* and Jeremy knew, or may have known.

"Really?"

"Really."

At that, Jeremy teetered, reached for the edge of the bar, which may have been slippery to his hindered grip, then he went straight back, legs folding at the knees and knees pointing out—a circumstance Jeremy seemed not to register immediately. He took the stool down with him, and he seemed to land more softly, rolling on his outerly arched back, his expression blankly foolish.

I rose. It really was getting harder and harder to enjoy a quiet, maundering drink here.

"Did you hit your head?" I asked, looking down and watching him air-grasp his way up.

"I did not hit my head," he announced with Warner Brothers dignity.

He laughed at himself, or the bar, or for all I knew me. He laughed, cutely, vulnerably.

"Awesome then," I said.

"Fucking hell, I didn't hit my head."

Then he was tender, just within emotional reach, but I didn't help him since Davy—who was much prettier—flew out from behind the bar and gripped one arm, and said, "You okay?"

I helped him into a taxi, had another beer, then walked home. Thinking about how things ended here. How they started here—young writers and artists getting started—then ended here.

"You were the first one I met here," said Rich in the facility. "But are you feeling stronger?"

Around Christmas in his Old Town house, alone, Hank had reached for his scooter chair and miscalculated the distance between his grip and the handles, then fallen. He'd lain there for eight hours, falling asleep, waking up, pissing and shitting himself, languishing in pain, in a daze he could only remember for its daziness, until landscapers entered the house early the next day to ask for their check and found him unconscious on the hard tile: "I really believed I was a goner!"

Hank was eighty-five and the first to welcome Rich to Key West, when New York hadn't only become too expensive but also a loud show tune of itself. Brooklyn was a disappointment.

Hank had helped Rich grow up by taking his writing seriously, by saying he mattered.

Never before this moment had Rich believed he mattered less. He was nobody, nowhere.

Rich said, his heart sinking, his eyes almost wetting up, "You look pretty damn great."

Long silences between things said, between ideas conveyed, in the silent rehab facility.

Hank lay partly erect in his hospital bed, sleepy, his eyes still glittering but fixedly lazy, and said, his voice hushed and hoarse, "I'm glad to hear you say that. I'm okay. Yet I reached a terrible conclusion this morning. It happened— it came about when—I was talking to the social workers and therapists. Matt was here, as always. And I realized that my situation is a lot worse than I thought." Not stopping to swallow or gather his thoughts he continued: "A lot worse . . ."

Hank gazed stiffly and tightly as though the realization was still coming farther into view.

Hank laughed croakily, poor Hank, whose situation repelled Rich and demoralized him.

Because the vinyl-padded visitors' chair was piled with leg braces and workout clothes, Rich had taken the only available seat, Hank's wheelchair—and Rich said, "You're laughing!"

"I wonder what in the world else there is to do."

Rich had lost no one. He was a middle-class example of the middle-class son for whom nothing had gone wrong yet in his family. His parents seemed healthy. His siblings had children and even though his writing life wasn't working out for him he had hope, he had his health. And even though he was questioning whether or not he should stay in Key West for much longer, he at least was comfortable with the idea of staying for a while. His future was unsure, but whatever it was he was fairly certain he had one. He had his mornings to drink coffee in bed and read. He'd stashed some money from his grandfather's trust and could eat bean soup and be perfectly cool.

When he'd met Hank, Rich was trying to write like it was still the nineteenth century. He was looking for a subject, and Hank had reminded him that Rich's family was his subject. The usual normal, he'd encouraged, could only result in the finding of the unpredicted weirdnesses.

Hank was the only mentor Rich had ever known. Out of guilt he'd studied engineering.

"Don't concentrate too much on oldies like Melville and Hawthorne," Hank had said.

Now the books Hank had on his hospital tray table were open face-down, and he stared at the TV screen which was full of housewives reality shows, not even the news. Gardening shows.

The books weren't much more ambitious, gardening memoirs and potboiler novels.

Rich said, "What are you reading?"

"Basically nothing. Can't focus, don't even feel like trying . . ."

Not the Hank he'd known, who'd once almost been Rich's lover. Hank was a dynamo, a storehouse of memories, and more interesting memories, than Rich had banked. Yet now Hank's memories and sentences and words themselves were diffuse and dragged out, words useless, too.

And Rich said, "I'm sorry you're not feeling your usual wonderful, erudite self."

Rich smiled broadly, but his smile was out of Hank's peripheral.

"Okay . . ." said Hank hoarsely, his talk now racing raggedly with his labored breathing.

Rich was biking up almost daily to the hospital and his heart was breaking slowly. But usually, get Hank onto the past—anything could spark these recollections and soliloquies—and he was off again, resplendent, fluent, steadily grabbing at the bits, saying at the television, "That woman's house on the California coast reminds me of Nonie Phipps's place on Capri when I was working at Spoleto in Italy—which must have been about '55. Everyone knew her husband, the conductor, was gay—Tommy Schippers. Nonie knew, no one *didn't* know. But the last time—I saw—Tommy Schippers he was at—Sloan Kettering. This shriveled-up old, little. Guy. Yellow head to. Toe. There was an elevator for patients and he was getting on holding the door looking at me—waiting to see if I, see—recognized him. I said his name, he smiled. Doors—started—closing. He put his hand out to open them, toddled out, said he was fine. I said I hadn't asked. So we laughed and talked about Spoleto days. We started talking about Menotti and said those were good times. Then he got back on the fucking elevator and he was dead in a week."

Rich strained to hear, but thought he'd gotten it all.

Rich said, "Do you mind if I mute the TV? It's kind of hard to hear you."

"Oh, I don't care," said Hank waving feebly with a dry pale paddle-hand.

"Has Matt been in today already?" said Rich innocently—not sure if Hank knew.

"This morning. For my meeting. About my future. Which doesn't look so good now."

"I see. I'm so sorry. I'm worried. I'm sure Matt's worried, too. He loves you so much."

Hank waved his hand feebly again, paused, and composed himself, trying to sit up a bit.

Did Hank know about Rich and Matt? The mind in an ailing body could function fine.

"I thought I was going on two things this spring. A Nordic fjord cruise and then Rome in the spring. I was going to go. In a wheelchair. I might still, but it doesn't look so good today."

The breathless speech, which killed Rich, who was withdrawing now thinking of Matt.

"I'm so sorry, Hank."

Hank started to fall asleep between the words, in cushy, ascending silences. Just with the air conditioning, maybe the comfort of knowing the bed next to him had been abandoned a week ago. Then Hank woke and said, "I thought I was in Nantucket there for a minute. Am I still?"

"Not that I know of, but Henry Givens was just here, author of *Peggy: A Real Class Act*."

Hank tittered meekly, appreciatively.

Then: "When I first moved here there wasn't anybody. Just—good old Tennessee."

Rich got up and held his hand. He moved around the clutter and kissed Hank's head and said, "I'll see you soon, okay? I'll let you sleep but I'll be back tomorrow, all right, Hank?"

"Oh, I long for it," said Hank without opening his eyes. "I have a therapy in an hour so I just need to rest." He laughed a little again and added, "I'll be back from Nantucket in a flash."

Rich biked back down taking the causeway and then cleaving to the bayside. And looking beyond the boats to see if he could glimpse the Gulf, which he just could, just, and the wind was strong. He winced into it, his shades filming up from the salty wind. When he got to Old Town he let himself in through the garden gate, and there was Matt at Hank's desk, going over figures. The insurance was fucked-up but Matt, now Hank's legal husband, was taking it a figure at a time.

"Hi there."

"Hi there."

"How was he?"

"Dreamy. But okay. I thought he was good remembering things. Basically cheerful."

"Good. Don't let that go too long and deep in your head. We're at the end here, babe."

"I know, but I don't like to hear that. Maybe that's just the Methodism talking."

The dog, Chewy, came in flashing his pale yellow-lab tail, and Matt pulled Rich to him.

They kissed.

"I don't know what I'd do without you in all this," said Matt, who was twenty years older but strong and mature and in the fullness of his life, and went slack in the younger one's arms.

They closed the door to the bedroom against Chewy and had sex freely. For the first time since Greenpoint, when he'd had a buddy called Josh, Rich thought of it as making love, although he knew he wasn't the only one for Matt, who had an American Airlines pilot and a Cuban doctor in the romantic docket, too. "I guess I'm at the age of shit or get off the pot," Matt had told Rich, and yet Rich had never much considered Matt's age—Rich dying for a good and enduring love.

Then he could go back to Ocala and see his family.

I'M UP ON the deck of the rental in the dark when Jeremy sends me a text:

Hey u out?

Been out almost my whole life.

Smart ass. Need an escort for my first time at Fantasy House.

K. Meet you in thirty mins?

Cool.

I bike over. He's sitting in the lobby already checked in with his day pass.

We shake hands, half-hug, slap-embrace. He's not taking any chances.

I check in and we go to the locker room. I get naked and don't care about my body. He strips down to his shiny black boxer briefs and I say, "You're getting in the hot tub like that?"

"Yep."

We turn out to be the only ones in there.

"This is going in my story," I say.

"You can't write about this. I'm dating a guy up in Boston."

"Okay. My mouth is shut."

"Asshole. Don't detract from my romantic life. I just want a boyfriend that likes me."

"No problem."

Then he's sitting in the hot water in his underwear and he's on his phone. He shows me his new boyfriend, a theology student in Brookline, and I say, "Cute. What area of theology?"

"His name is Valentin. All I know is he's French but not Catholic."

"Huguenot, probably. He about your age?"

"Younger."

He cherishes the pic briefly, then puts his phone on his towel on the bench behind the hot tub, and I decide this trip is engineered to make me jealous, rub it in, remind himself he's alive.

"Wait," I say, "have you guys ever even met?"

The jets are firing all around the walls of the tub and

the chlorine smell is strong, and he's not only wearing his underwear but his Poindexter specs, too. One jet massages my lower back.

He blinks behind the foggy lenses, sitting across from me and letting a jet massage him.

Jeremy's looking at me as though to confirm what he already knew: I'm not for him.

It sort of hurts, but the jets massage me, and there's more where he came from, right?

We get out and dry off and go to the bar for drinks. He's quiet.

I say, "That's okay, you don't have to babysit me."

"Really?"

"Really."

"I'm just suddenly so tired. I'm gonna call a taxi, if that's okay."

Then I'm alone. Something makes me stay for hours. I go up into the dark room and I do some groping. I jerk off looking at the overhead porn. Nobody else comes in and I fall asleep and I wake up in what feels like dramatic silence. The porn, sound turned down as usual, is rote.

I get dressed and turn in my lock. The light is coming up as I bike to the other side of the island, a mixture of sad and joyous. There's always tomorrow just as there was a yesterday.

The fronds of the palms rattle. I stop in some bushes behind the big bank parking lot on Catherine to pee, then continue. I get to the cottage. I see the front door's open, the place dark inside.

I turn on the lights and call out for Perry and check the two main rooms, but no Perry.

I unlock and get on my bike and circle the neighborhood and find him walking unsteadily without his cane, pausing where the trees obscure the streetlights, confused, taking his time.

I'm straddling my bike, then dismount and gently set it down on the cement curb.

He utters, "Oh," sensing me there, hearing the rattle of metal.

"Perry, sweetheart?"

He doesn't turn, is hunched, shoulders slightly rolled forward, and he says, "Scott?"

A clutch in my throat—he knows me.

"Yes, darling."

"Oh," he repeats, putting his hand out, not turning, "there you are. Hey. Can you help me?"

The Book About Perry

My agent, Stella Marsh, buzzed me to ask if I was making any progress.

I shouldn't have taken the call. To start, I was anxious. I hadn't worked all day.

Actually, Stella wasn't my agent yet, she'd merely agreed to read a second version of the memoir I was writing. Foolishly, I told her it all seemed to be going fine. I feared she must be hearing the background house music of the outdoor gay bar where I sat, and the ambient, occasionally raucous, gay male laughter resounding as I set down my beer.

"Where *are* you?" Stella said in a quizzed upspeak.

"We're in Key West," I said. "Everything's cheek to jowl down here, pretty much. The guesthouse where Perry and I are staying has a garden bar behind it."

"I've never been," she said. "Is it nice?"

"Kind of touristy and crowded, but we love it."

A parched-throated queen several places down from me cackled.

I wondered if she thought that was Perry in need of a glass of water, watching TV.

"I'm sitting here on the front porch working," I added for verisimilitude, stepping away from the bar. "The guesthouse is right on Fleming, a block from downtown."

I thought of her desk in her mile-high office in midtown, though I'd never seen it.

Boys splashed playing volleyball in the pool.

"Basically, I work in earplugs."

"Ha ha. A lot of my authors say they thrive on distraction."

I had the sensation that as I spoke them I was casting my words into a void, and that while standing on the edge of that void only I could hear them echo as they wheeled downward, and that I might keel dizzily forward after them—and I gave a rough laugh.

I'd met her in New York at one of those parties where everyone was worried but acted relaxed, pretending to take an easeful pace in social life and enjoying the free booze before going home to fall into bed and wake up early with the desire to stick a fist in their mouths. Briefly, often, I felt sorry for the hustling literary agents of New York with their sky-high office overhead, their hunger for the bestseller—not just a *succès d'estime,* like what I thought I was writing. A blockbuster, ha ha. I was too much of a minnow for top seasoned contract chef Stella Marsh to fry. This came to me as the draft of IPA I'd been swishing around in my mouth I allowed to swill and sizzle down my throat.

My memoir-in-progress, tentatively titled *The Husband* (about my life with my older husband, the author Perry Knight), was meant to describe what a devoted mate I'd been in our twenty-some years together. This given our open relationship and given his health problems, which had become legion in his older age. *But who would care?* Stella had back then challenged me when I'd done an unconvincing verbal soft-shoe, what they also call the elevator pitch.

(Being any kind of artist in New York is vertiginous business.)

I'd gone home, no doubt like others, demoralized but lit for a long winter's nap.

Christmas had made its gaudy appearance, barely noticed by Perry and me, then New Year's, and soon we were heading into Presidents' Day. I continued to write in my unrepresented vainglory, putting up my imagined shingle, I JUST WORK HERE, which was one of Perry's best pieces of advice to me when we'd first met and I was just a pup.

Then it was announced that Perry had won the first

PEN/Richard Yates Award for Career Achievement in American Fiction. It was noticed from afar in *The Guardian* and *Le Monde*. *CBS Sunday Morning* covered it, although the folks at CBS seemed to have a hard time framing this author of nearly thirty books about being gay in America, where it already had become boring for half the TV audience—and for the other half occasioned irritated American Christians to get up, pour more coffee, and get another cinnamon roll.

"Who was that?"

"Another gay guy."

"Boy, and it's not like there's anybody there asking them to shut up about it."

"Libtards."

"Good-ass breakfast, hon."

Stella contacted me through Facebook messaging.

Folks deride Facebook, but it's where I've gotten most of my best contacts and unpaid assignments. Without mentioning Perry's PEN/Richard Yates, Stella asked me how much of my book I'd written, and how soon she could have a look at it. Stella was the first not to conjure any of those magic, pat phrases of regret like: "There is much to admire in these pages. And yet despite the often assured and skillful writing, I'm afraid I'll have to let this one go." Or: "I'll bet that at some point, if it hasn't done so already, this piece will find a home." "I think I should just step aside." And: "Of course, there's every possibility that I may one day regret my final agonized decision, but unfortunately the market is very tight at this time, and the economics of publishing being what they are, I need to pass on this, let you go out and incinerate it in a grill, and then flush the ashes."

Literary subtext being everything.

Rejection letters sounded like nothing more than condolence notes, or bread-and-butters to the hostess whose buffet you upset by drunkenly walking away with one corner of the linen cloth wrapped around your ankle, dragging the flame-warmed chafing dishes, heirloom saucepots, silver salvers, expensive china, and two hundred pounds of engraved flatware along with it. But Stella had been more tentatively reassuring in her acceptance. Brightly poker-faced, even.

"It's a bit prolix," she'd replied, learning that one I thought at Hotchkiss or Yale.

A couple paragraphs down she concluded, "But these are all minor quibbles . . ."

My heart sat up straight.

I remembered from the book party this confident procurer of thoroughbred talents with her long, smooth, freshly blonded hair, who did not drink, smiled at your little jokes and attempts at wit, and sometimes winked at you, protruding the tiny tip of her tongue.

The last thing I wanted to do at that point was disappoint Stella or Perry, who was trying on his tux before

I sent it out to the cleaners in preparation for the PEN ceremony when I came in with the news, which made him proud.

After the acceptance, and Perry's light, funny speech on the disorienting marvels of Kawabata and Tanizaki, we exchanged a kiss and tears and went to the Oyster Bar.

"You got your ticket?" he said.

"I got my ticket."

"Well, darling."

Perry and I checked in every day.

As of today, I hadn't heard from Stella since St. Patrick's.

"Well," said Stella, "so you're working."

"Every day."

"May I ask, then, how soon?"

"Within weeks."

"Let's say," she chirped, consulting a mental calendar, "by Holy Thursday?"

"Is that the same as Maundy Thursday, the Thursday before Easter?"

"I think so. I'm just kidding, it's the Thursday before Easter."

I had no idea what that was this year, but I wasn't the one to stand on ceremony.

I knew we were in the middle of Lent. I made a note to Google Holy Thursday.

We hung up, and I went back to the bar and lifted my lukewarm beer shakily.

There was near my corner of the bar under the tiki hut a young man, a boy really, who'd just said good-bye to some older gents. His straw hair stuck up—he'd been cured by the subtropical sun, and when he smiled at me the darkness of his features lifted away.

"Man, have you ever sailed?" he said.

"I haven't. Well, not for more than a few hours at a time. I grew up in Florida."

"Man, you've gotta sail. You've never been on the outside of the Gulf Stream?"

"What do you mean?"

"Say you're on a boat, I live on a boat. My boyfriend has a boat. He's a fucking asshole, but I love him. He's got this seventy-foot job, we're docked at a berth on Stock Island. Do you know what you do if you want a boat and don't have one? You go down to the Lesser Antilles, and that's where them wives lose their nerve. That's exactly where they give up on their husbands. Start at Nantucket, or wherever— and by the time their husbands have them down in the Lesser Antilles, it's all over. Ladies just can't keep on, man."

"You mean they quit, they give up, stop sailing?"

"It was just a pipe dream, and their wives just want to go home, man, fucking go home."

"But what was that about the Gulf Stream?"

"Have you seen it? It's wild! It's indescribable. Lemme try to describe it . . ."

I was remembering Hemingway's description of it in

To Have and Have Not (else it was *Islands in the Stream*), the welling, rushing masculine stem of it, like a great pure vein of nature, pushing, flowing, threatening everything in its way, like an intimidatingly large erect penis.

And I said, "It's like a deep-blue, almost purple?"

"Naw, nothing like that, but it's immense, it's terrifying. We have a cat on board . . ."

His arms swung out and flung up and his eyes were wild, terrified. He was past drunk.

"Yeah," I said, "okay."

"The cat," he went on, "she's all over, she's freaking out. It's like a wall. You know how they described the tsunami, like in the Pacific? That's what it looks like, it's just its own fucking thing, and you can feel, like it's coming for you, like it's a wave, like a wall, and you're heading right the hell into it. Terrifying. Cat's afraid, then up on deck I'm looking out—dark and high! Scariest, worst thing you've ever seen . . ."

He seemed to be the best describer of the situation, despite his histrionics. He had awe, a thing I admired—from a natural boy, a young man whose greatest nature required much alcohol to get itself out of him. The slice of smile, the wild straw hair.

I said, "You mean it's raised, higher than the water around it?"

"It's more than that," he said, letting his arms rest, then taking a sip of scotch and water.

"I can't imagine."

I said this because I was confused.

"No, you just head into it. You know the Bermuda Triangle in lore? That's the Stream."

I was impressed by *lore,* seemingly beyond his years, and wondered where he'd picked that up. But then I usually underestimated the educations of younger people.

"The Stream, it's extreme. It's terrifying. Mainly because it just seems so—unexpected."

I smiled to rhyme with his enthusiasm, and said, "Good word, *unexpected.*"

"No, but wait, man."

When he was done describing the near-insurmountability of the Gulf Stream, I took him further in. He was a compact marvel, as insurmountable and indescribable as the Stream. But I'd been in the near shade under the tiki roof for hours, drinking, and his summery hair was the last thing on his mind. I didn't have to care about the Gulf Stream as much as he did. He was already off on top of it in his mind, and I could just ride along over the high rushing edge of it, and probably not have to keep up. I could just sort of follow, nodding.

I said, "What's your name."

"Arthur. Why? Man, I love your look, I just love the way you look. Jewish, right?"

"No."

"I love your beautiful neck, it's so perfect. I'd like to get my lips on it."

"Thanks. You can, later. Well, but it's covered in beard, salt and pepper."

"What I love! I'd like to get my lips on it."

"You're way too young for me. Is that what your boyfriend has, too?"

"Fuck you. Don't talk about my boyfriend, he's an asshole."

"All right, all right."

He had two-thirds of a cocktail and he, with crippled motions, this debilitated movement that said his spinal activity was close to shutting down, but not quite yet, grabbed into his right pocket and hauled out wads of cash as well as a piece of folded, crumpled paper that fell onto the deck under the tiki roof, and he raised his arm and signaled to the bartender's back. But it was the bartender's back, and not his front.

"Hey! Hey! Chris! Billy! Whatever your name is!"

The bartender turned but didn't identify himself. He narrowed his eyes. At the other end, he was talking to locals—regulars who could joke with Chris and call him a whore and share their slutty secrets about last night or recent carnal, nocturnal histories. They looked surprised that the delectable sun-blond Arthur should signal him in a fashion so haughty. But the bartender stepped over to us and managed a tolerant tone: "Yes?"

"One more of this shit," said Arthur.

Then I realized Arthur had two different drinks going,

ignoring them both. They were already there, he didn't see them or else loathed him, and he wanted a fresh one.

"Another margarita, rocks, no salt?" said Chris the bartender.

The kid didn't respond but looked at me and said, "I want a kiss, man. Give me a kiss, okay?"

Which made my day.

"No," I said, wrinkling my brow, "I don't want to kiss you."

"Jesus Christ! One. Then fuck me. I want you to fuck me. Over behind the fire pit."

"I've already had too much to drink," I said, which was true, there'd be no performance out of me today, and maybe no work, and he waved me off staying planted.

The drink came and the kid shoveled the wad of bills toward the bartender, picked up his drink, and said to him, "Jesus Christ. Give me a towel. I want a towel. I wanna go in. This guy won't fuck me. He won't kiss me. I'd like a towel, if you don't mind."

Chris gave the kid a towel, from his fund of towels stowed in a hutch just under the tiki beams, and Arthur, his limbs all akimbo, such terra-cotta limbs, stepped down off the wood planking under the tiki roof and onto the cement skirt of the pool and hot tub. I was ready for my next beer, but by then the bartender had returned to the locals, his back to me. Arthur removed his bathing suit, all he'd been wearing to begin with, and made his way down the cement steps of the hot tub daintily, holding the chrome railing with one hand and the margarita with the other. Then in up to his chest. After a sip he set his drink on the edge next to his towel and plunged under, staying there, his long hair fanning gold and brown in the light blue, bubbles popping on the surface. Briefly, he had an audience in us all (all five of us despite the two-for-ones and the pretty day, a break in the cold front that had lasted for days). I knew that I did want Arthur, but maybe not as much as I wished I could see the Gulf Stream, the looming murderous wall of it, if I weren't too poor to get on a boat and do this—or maybe to have both without the boyfriend on board, that would be even better. But anything, I knew, would be better than having to write.

When the bartender came back over, he waved his cigarette and got me a new plastic cup and filled it with draft from the tap, saying, "She's a hot mess. I would've kicked her hot ass out a long time ago, except she's decorative. When they're hot and decorative they get a blank check to a point, that's just standard procedure, but otherwise she'd have been out on her hot ass hours ago."

"I'll keep an eye on him," I said, giving him a two-dollar tip for a two-dollar beer, and he sneered, but cutely, as if to say we were in the same snarky, joking zone. He reached up and dropped the bills in the galvanized tip bucket hanging from the rafters.

He went away back to the locals, and I got a new line to

help reinvigorate the start of my third chapter. I was confident about the first two, less so about the next two. *When he and I first met . . .* my thought about Perry began, and considered how he and I had first met in Paris. I thought more strictly about Perry at this point, what he was thinking, how he was doing, then wondered if our friend Beau was managing all right with him up in New York. Beau's old beau was in Costa Rica for a month, visiting family, and they'd given their apartment to friends they owed favors to and the whole thing had worked out cleanly. The winter had been another erratic one in New York, starting late, as though the wheel of the year were wobbling on its once-sturdy axis, Christmas Day temperatures topping out at seventy degrees. But now up there, icy systems were sliding down from the Arctic, not lingering long but imprisoning Perry for days at a time. With Beau, Perry could stay inside safe and let Beau do the running-out, but then Perry didn't get exercise. A walk to his favorite deli on the corner threatened a slip and fall. But to stay a shut-in for days—that was no good, either. Still, I was grateful to Beau, who'd moved on gracefully since I'd tried to finesse him romantically after our first stilted sex over two evenings fifteen years ago, when Perry was still well and traveled to Europe by himself on some festival's dime. Good relationships could become perfunctorily cozy over time; they lasted because they'd started good. Something good in them remained, a true love.

Then I heard a languid, "He's been under for a while."

"Yeah, pretty good long while . . ."

I looked over and saw Arthur's figure fuzzy and below the surface of the hot tub, his arms spread and his legs bent slightly at the knees as though his feet were operating vehicle pedals.

But they rushed over and fished him out. With his limp-limbed help they dragged him out of the chlorinated water and laid him on the cement. He didn't cough or sputter. I couldn't see his eyes. Arthur lay in the sun, hair slicked down around his head, then he turned on his side and went into the fetal, his front to us. His penis was plump, pink, nested in its glistening gold bush. He scrunched further into a tight fetal, his shoulders and chest expanding with breath.

Things went back to dull normal. I'd made the right decision by not making any at all.

I was getting old. Getting older meant not regretting your most recent decisions, too much. It meant letting go of the possibility of imminent sexual adventure because of your responsibilities, which suddenly I remembered I had, and would forthwith dispatch.

I WAS STAYING in an informal, unmarked guesthouse that didn't advertise in order to keep costs down. In case anyone asked, the only people staying there were Ham's friends and family. And in the evening come-and-go social activity on the front porch of Ham's old Queen Anne things felt like a gathering of souls thrown together to ride out the storm of needful corner-cutting and aging. I was the oddball that month, the lone gay guest who was a writer (everyone was nice, even curious about that).

Ham was a cheerful gay man in his upper sixties or lower seventies who'd bought in after Hurricane Wilma, when island real estate had drastically ebbed. He and a young friend, Eduardo, licked the place into shape, yanking up rotting floor planks, replacing the broken and moldy lengths of gingerbread, clobbering lathe and plaster to reconfigure rooms once accommodating the dreams and desires of a ghosty dowager ship-captain's daughter. The rooms were nicely furnished, exceedingly clean, and had snugly glazed windows and ceiling fans hung from high ceilings on long stems. Ham took checks—at half the rate of real guesthouses. It was a sweet secret, with access to a well-stocked kitchen where I could microwave my processed mac and cheese. Simplified, unhealthy dinners were my boon: I could ignore Perry's exacting diet. I was indulging down here in every single way, with the understanding that I must write. I had to finish the book about us. The deadline was now real and I wanted to capitalize on Perry's fame among a rapidly dying readership: gay males. His first crop of readers had died of AIDS a while ago. Now old age was hacking away with scythe precision at their survivors, but only those who still read. We were talking about a pretty small audience. It occurred to me sometimes that my once proven skill (I'd published one book) might itself carry me across the finish line. But I'd published the first book while Perry was still in visibly good health, upright, able to take care of himself. My courage flagged.

In order to have faith at all in finishing and believing sufficiently in the book, I needed to be alone. I bet myself that at a hundred dollars a night I'd be motivated to get it over with. Stella was the spirit here, the captain's daughter waiting for Papa's ship to come gliding into harbor.

The place was cleanly spooky, haunted in the first half of the day by spirits hanging out in their rooms watching TV or reading. Usually I'd catch one of them in the kitchen preparing food to drag back to the shadows. But Ham and Eduardo, when I saw them at all, appeared suddenly in the kitchen for longer, finishing last night's Publix or Winn-Dixie fried chicken, cleaning up their leftover coleslaw and potato salad between bouts of yard work or other outdoor projects, talking a halting, hesitant Spanish. They were always cheerful but usually cheerfully silent together. I rather envied them.

Eduardo, so far as I could tell, was not Ham's lover, only an assistant hired in Homestead on the mainland where orchids were grown for grocery chains and where Ham leased land to the flower growers for their greenhouses. Eduardo had been sent back to Guatemala by ICE; his electrician father had raised five thousand dollars to smuggle him back. In the morning, when I came into the, again, very nice kitchen looking for a mug of the coffee I made in my bathroom, Eduardo might be at the breakfast counter eating cornflakes and pretending to be able to laugh at my jokes. He set to work helping Ham clean the rooms of those who had checked out, yet most were in for the season. Or trimming the coconuts off the two-story palms or raking up the green, walnut-like pods falling from the six-story kapok tree out back. It was the time of the year when the kapok shed everything, leaves and all, and its worst offense was dropping the pods violently, like base-balls on the tin roof with every shiver of wind, though when it was time for the ripened pods to drop they didn't wait for an excuse. Other guests were driven to distrac-tion by the pod-dropping. It made porch-talk get going in a hurry while they waited for the effects of their beer or wine to overcome them, when the laughter started. I did most of my writing on the far end of the porch in my Adirondack, my Mac in my lap, a glass of wine by my side. The Adirondack's opposite had been dragged off to the other end of the porch to join the party. One man did not need an Adirondack. He was in a powered wheelchair, and because there was a ramp leading from the sidewalk up to this porch, he didn't need his wife's help negotiating the tight corners and narrow passes of the gallery—which is what Ham called the wraparound porch. Steven could lower a ramp in the side of a retrofitted van parked out front in the street, haul himself up in the chair, and park it where the driver's seat had been removed behind the wheel. The ramp, like everything of Steven's, including his mood, was automatic. He was friendly even when he did not drink, even at nine in the morning before heading off to grocery-shop the big-box stores in the strips on the cheaper end of the island. His younger wife, Melissa, would appear for the first time of the day sometime around noon, wearing Bermuda shorts, neatly fitted tees, and white canvas Keds, and drink hot tea and pace the high-gloss gray boards of the gallery.

Not only were they all mostly friendly, they respected my creative time and kept to each other and themselves when they saw or heard me tapping on my keyboard. I worked mostly on the front porch, accustomed to working in the back lounge of a Chelsea gay bar in New York. I needed scenery and yes, distraction, though not too much. I wore earplugs but mostly out of habit from writing during happy hour.

I was establishing a new routine at Ham's. I got home from the bar about four in the afternoon, as usual. Happy hour on the gallery hadn't started—and I was buzzed sufficiently not to start panicking yet. I'd Googled Holy Thursday. I had eighteen days to polish anywhere from seventy-five to a hundred pages about my life (so far) with a novelist who wrote mostly about homosexuality and whose novels few had read or even heard of. My book wasn't inspirational and wasn't meant to be, though inspiration and redemption sold the best. It was, I thought, funny, original. In it I stored funds of anecdotes on French conversations gone amusingly wrong in Paris, where I had met my great and occasionally bawdy hero-wordsmith, as well as hospital humor—gallows ironies, as I liked to think of them. In the past several years Perry had made hospitalization an avocation that was near-routine if always surprising and harrowing. Do you know who the worst offenders in a hospital setting are as far as smoking is concerned? Respiratory therapists. It was difficult for a man as hardheaded as Perry, who once smoked and drank and drugged with a postwar aplomb akin to the Beats', to take orders from overweight and freely self-admittedly diabetic nurses. The respiratory therapists come in and set up their sulfurous misting masks and begin going over last night's Fox News coverage. They love Fox. There it is on Perry's chart: HIV, history of strokes, double bypass. The therapists get a laugh at the expense of patients, their inmates as it were. They just got their president and can say what they want. Their tattletale prattle is unheard, and uncommented on, because the patient is masked, half under from drugs.

"There are no laws in hospitals," one respiratory therapist told me, "just rules that can or cannot be enforced." (Which—what do you do with that? Do libertarians educate our fund of respiratory therapists? I know that if a patient, like Perry, got tired of getting his respiratory therapy, and clawed his mask off, the Fox-loving therapist just shrugged and looked away.)

Mostly, as you know, waiting around in hospitals is grindingly dull, but you can always, by listening, find something to write down. In Perry's last hospitalization, I had fallen asleep in my chair at the foot of his bed and woken up in a dream state to voices, a series of voices suggesting a stream of consciousness about the America we'd inherited.

Overnight, as quickly as health could turn into infirmity.

The same is true in Key West when you hear the loud-speakered tour guide announcing his memorized facts to the tourists riding in the cars of the passing street choo-choo:

"Supposedly, in 1513 Juan Ponce de León landed on these shores and found nothing but acres of piled bones everywhere, the savage graveyard of Indians who'd since bugged out."

The tourists who hear this story delight in the piratical quality of the tour guides' perhaps apocryphal version of things, then no doubt obliterate it with alcohol and deep-fried seafood in the comfort of their island accommodations. They smoke cigars evoking an old Mafia-purchased Havana; they come to renew their marital vows, if more racily, but mostly they come to forget—just as I always do whenever I land in Key West.

So the island was America, or the outcroppings of it, just as the hospital had been a microcosm of it, and I wanted my book to get all that down. I was exiting the suburbs, the past.

Take your time with this, I'd told myself. Relax and dissolve yourself in saline breezes, get lost in the moment of creativity. It had always worked before. Already the taint of rejection had colored my resignation. I wanted to go back to my native form of the short story, which had stood me in passable stead. In my first collection, several had been set in Key West, which I had called somewhere in one of them "a small Southern town with bohemian values": in short, the town in the South I hadn't been raised in but later out of nostalgia had wanted to find. I'd had lots of teenage sex up in north Florida, swanning briefly in a mall bathroom stall with an older boy before returning to my roots as a brain-dead immersive Baptist-lite. I was putting all of this into my memoir, too, but *The Husband* lacked some credibility, some greater outrageous indulgence of the truth. It needed fancy. I got into Ham's Queen Anne on Fleming Street that afternoon, and first things first made sure my laptop was charged, and I went into my room to take a massive beer leak.

Two of the rooms on the first floor shared a bathroom in the hallway, mine and that of an older woman from the Lake Erie coast of Ohio whose own room was half the size of mine—a glorified closet with a single bed that matched, as I imagined, the compact nature of her idyllic, modest widowhood.

Gloria usually napped at this hour, or at least I never heard the television or any sounds at all from inside her room next to mine—and I rapped confidently on our shared bathroom's door.

From within I heard her holler: "I'm in my panties!"

I had a long wait so I texted Perry, who sometimes called text messages emails. Like me, Perry had come a long way technologically, but he sometimes confused these two things. And he often left his phone at home, or misplaced it. In the hospital, as he was recovering from his heart attack and surgery, coming out of the anesthesia and painkillers, he'd asked me to bring him his phone, which he'd rarely ever used. It had been stolen overnight while he was smack under the fentanyl still and only slow emerging. I had reported the phone stolen and hospital security sent someone to interview me and tell me I could fill out a form to get money for a replacement, which I never did. I was busy already with insurance forms and appeals to move him to an acute rehab where he could get his physical therapy and come home and be relatively independent and start living a normal life again. I hadn't called him today, I remembered. My groin burned, and this urgency was too much like the urgency I put on myself regarding Perry. He was probably napping. Could I just relax? The weather was milder today. It had been cold and awful and until this morning I'd gone around town in a fleece jacket, a light hair shirt. Then I remembered the outdoor john, the one with a wood-louvered door, out on the side gallery, facing the empty pool and unoccupied deck of the boutique hotel next door. The view was obscured by shrubs and tropical trees, but even when Ham's guesthouse was quiet and no one was stirring out here, I wouldn't sit on the toilet to use it. Anyway, it would have been too cold on most days to pull my pants down and sit there in the sluicing draft. A year ago I'd gotten down on my knees and called on my knowledge of CPR learned in junior high to resuscitate Perry on the floor, the memory of the health-class lessons and practice coming back to me. Technically he'd died, but I'd pushed myself, maybe out of fear of losing him or being accused of not having done enough. He'd almost died a second time, of sudden shock, when they got him into the ambulance. They were giving him an EKG and the medics had called from the back to the driver and me up front, "It's hot, it's hot! Let's go!" The constant urgency about Perry, then. In *The Husband,* I was trying to get all that confusion and urgency down, but since it never went away I could never forget it, just like this peeing in Ham's forgotten and thus always clean john. And Perry had nearly died, then started to make a recovery but would never be the same. In *The Husband,* I was trying not to be myself but do a credible impersonation of myself with the ironic twist of an objectivity the reader might find offensive. The writer, like the alcoholic, thinks there's a way in which the cleverest of us can achieve this impersonation while coming out a perfectly nice guy, just a funnier one. I had to admit what a dick I was, getting bored and falling asleep while my husband lay wavering between fearful nod and almost-death, and it would only work if I were somehow charming. The book had to fucking entertain, and I thought of Stella, and all her cohort and colleagues, and I respected and at the same time felt sorry for them. Because literature was urgent, it was dire—but needed to be fun.

(Subsequently I'd read or heard anecdotally at some dinner party I was attending with the gradually recovering Perry that the memory of pain left us quickly, replaced by our version of the trauma, the Event, which we collapsed into a simplified form that did not necessarily match what had actually happened in the middle of things; this knowledge and my bladder haunted me now. This and Perry's memory of waking up in the hospital remembering the EMTs as a bunch of nice, if oversmiling, men all sheathed in a patterned linoleum. I needed to get to work.)

On the porch Gloria sat in one of the far-end Adirondacks reading the Bible that was open in her lap. I settled in an Adirondack on my end, opened my laptop, opened the document of *The Husband,* and scanned my text. Without too much pain or longing, I began to remove words like *harrowing,* reminding myself to show "harrowing" without using a pile-up of adjectives. No, the adjectives, I told myself, should be spare and reserved to describe the ambulance, the ambulance ride, the oddly hushed bustle of the emergency room, Perry's shifting hue throughout his trauma. The burly EMTs, the bulky nurses, the kind faces and admirable reserve of the doctors and intake personnel. I struck out their *preternatural grace* and, unfortunately, my favorite, their *uncannily inexorable yet compassionate resolve.* (But as one of my old writing teachers had said: "Murder your darlings.")

One note, typed in red, said:

Demonstrate desperate by undercutting it with medical precision, artful science, and above all, love!

I hatcheted and sutured like this for a while, almost incanting myself into the sensation of hovering above an unconscious Perry as the team worked beneath the ER's kliegs. I did my best work partially out of guilt's memory. I finished work on the second chapter and when I returned from the kitchen, where I'd exchanged my rinsed and racked juice glass for an iced-tea tumbler I filled to the brim with more white wine, some of Ham's guesthouse crew were assembling on the front porch, including Steven and Melissa. Steven had a nook for his beer on the right handle of his wheelchair, and Melissa held a glass of rosé and was taking the Adirondack opposite Gloria.

Melissa was saying, "Well, but wouldn't you want just a teensy-tiny bit of rosé?"

And Gloria then was replying, "I do think I would take half a glass."

Steven picked his bottled beer up from the wheelchair handle and waved it at me.

"Hello, hello!" he said. "Getting good work done?"

"Yes, yes," I said, smiling profusely and stupidly, even waving. "I am, in fact!"

Hunched toward my screen in my Adirondack, I was pretending to work. But I was more interested in how Melissa paused, smacking her lips, and commented that it was a new vintage to her, this rosé. Others smacked their lips, too, in sympathy.

I was so horny. Actually, all I could think about was going out, and soon, trying to fuck.

I did not want to feel middle-aged and middle-American, which, essentially, I was.

"Boy, I like it," said Gloria. "It's bubbly like pop. In Ohio—and I don't know how things are up your way in Michigan—they sell a variety of local wines, by which I mean wine made from locally grown grapes and bottled right there, particularly along Lake Erie. But are many of you the descendants of German immigrants, too? Because our wine-growing people along Lake Erie are the descendants of German immigrants." She prattled on like the author of a tourist brochure, or a set of self-published memoirs: "And in my family we swerve between two proud traditions of winegrowers and schoolteachers, which is what I am, a retired teacher, German on both sides."

"Us too, us too."

I wanted to listen to loud music, dance in place, drink cold beer, and talk to some boys.

The porch lights twitched to life. I hadn't quite yet noticed the sky's darkening.

I "knew" these people. I'd done time in Ohio as a grad student. Alcohol was a "naughty" necessity, something to whistle in the dark about and make light of. That was America, strangers reaching across a gulf, out of a learned, implicit obligation. Now magnify that ten times and you have the insanity of growing up in the South under a low-class Protestantism, not with the decent, sturdy rectitude of Lutheranism or German or Polish Catholicism. (Our kooky eyes, that gabby bullshit.) Even as the party on the porch advanced and they spoke bibulously, I was struck by the relative silences in between words. The talk was the usual twaddle (which of course I was just as capable of), but they were at least pretending to consider what they were saying. I glanced over.

Melissa looked at husband Steven, who fidgeted between sipping his bottled beer and touching the controls of his powered wheelchair and nudging it lightly so that it moved back and forth a little, rocking himself into submission to polite, ladyish talk.

Steven said, "So have I got this right, you were a public-school teacher too, and of what?"

Melissa interrupted him and said, "Steven was a public-school teacher in the UP. We still live in Newberry."

"Oh," said Gloria, tentatively, in a way that suggested cleverness, "what county's that?"

"Luce," replied Steven, nodding from his suddenly stilled wheelchair. "I did high school civics."

"Steven is writing his novel," said Melissa, and there was an important pause.

I remembered my parents' evaluations of Northerners—Yankees—as being icily diffident. This memory dilated as I listened to them haltingly getting on. Key West brought out the warmth in everybody, even Europeans, I found. But then it was the mention of a social participant's novel-writing that generally put the brakes on any conversation, in New York as well, since there was no sense of pity and mutual respect that could vouchsafe a potential failure like an American novelist's. It was largely uncomfortable, is what I'm saying. It even made me, a fiction writer no one had paid significant attention to following my first book's debut, *uncomfortable*—and it brought out a soft wine-enabled schadenfreude in me to witness after my considerable past failures, especially when I heard Gloria release a tight little tartly approving, "Hmm!," as though she wasn't sure whether or not to believe in another novel in the course of American literature. Or it was just the rosé.

"Steven's novel," Melissa announced, "is about the Michigan Twenty-fourth, who were a part of the Iron Brigade and suffered huge losses at McPherson's Ridge. Many don't know about all the black volunteers from Michigan at Gettysburg. I love his title, which is *The Wolverine.*"

(Another listening hobby of mine was to try to guess which political party strangers belonged to, although increasingly in Key West it was the Republican.)

I looked up from my screen and saw Steven wink at me in the yellowy anti-insect light.

"I like the title," declared Gloria flatly. "It really, what do they say, *zings.*"

"Doesn't it? That's what I think, too. But it's the writing that makes it, and the history."

I couldn't see Gloria's expression—hers was the Adirondack facing away from me—but I imagined her narrowing her eyes then widening them behind her butterfly-shaped frames, lifting her stenciled-on brows, when she said, "And what is that book you're reading, Melissa? I was a high school English teacher for tenth, eleventh, and twelfth grades. Now, I will tell you just how much I enjoyed teaching the likes of Dickens and Shakespeare. How I adored Shakespeare! The soliloquies of Hamlet, of Lady Macbeth! At the end I was being asked to teach books below that standard, and I confess I don't miss that. But at the same time, I do confess I don't miss the weather either."

"Screw the weather!" out came Melissa. "Although the summers."

"Oh, the summers!" declared Gloria. "The tomatoes, and the fruit!"

Steven let go of his controls, laughing—he laughed often and volubly—lifting his beer.

He said, "We're all here escaping the weather!"

"That's right," said Melissa, a little glumly, "gimme that good Key West winter weather."

I did not miss childhood. I didn't feel like thinking or writing about it.

"Sure can get cold back home," Gloria said, and I heard her titter.

They all had to laugh agreeably and approvingly, then Melissa cleared her throat, looked at me from across the way, then finished her second sip and said, "No, I'm reading a novel about Hadley. Gloria, you know Hadley, Hemingway's first wife? Well, she was his first wife."

"I didn't teach Hemingway. I confess to never having cared for him personally, and that's I'll admit just completely subjective. But what on earth do you mean by a novel about his wife?"

The rosé seemed to be making her more authoritative and daring and proud of her doubts.

"Hemingway lived right here," said Steven.

"Yeah, but not with Hadley," Melissa snapped.

Zipporah, a woman with russet corkscrews twisting

and falling down her back, ran an art gallery next door selling Haitian canvases, colorful scenes of lively and populous village life, and came home now leading her frisky rat terrier, Jean-Marie, on his leash. Zipporah and Jean-Marie made do up in the single attic-size room on the third floor, yet what they lost in living area they gained by having sole access to the widow's walk, with its commanding view of Fleming Street. Ham kept the shapely and quaintly hand-turned railings of the widow's walk rot-free and painted radium white—and even on the bleakest days the widow's walk was the first feature you noticed at 614. Zipporah stopped to say hello to our inmates, doing what I thought of as just checking-in since she never tarried long—though I will say that she seemed to know everyone's name.

She tried to get in a joke and a laugh early each time. Jean-Marie tested the extent of his leash, padding over in my direction and heeling paces away from me to study a potted palm next to the front door, a wan vegetable excrescence that was fading from the recent colder days. Jean-Marie wasn't one of those ungainly, panting, tongue-hanging types but, like his owner, kept an un-needy, resting dignity. He couldn't quite help his curiosity, but briefly he side-eyed me as though disgusted—doubtless because Zipporah, who talked to him constantly, had taught him to loathe and pity me as a smoker. I generally smoked in the street, but as anyone who's never smoked or who, like me, has embarrassed himself trying to quit countless times knows, shit has a tendency to stink anywhere it hasn't been invited and to sink into unpredicted spaces, especially when the wind is unfavorable. Breezes in Key West seem always to be coming out of nowhere.

It made me want a cigarette, this Pavlov's dog's triggering loathing. Jean-Marie cocked one floppy ear back toward the others as he kept an eye on me: "You jonesing for a butt, bud?"

Zipporah gave her hooty chuckle at the others, winding her end of the leash once around her fist and tugging lightly on it, and said, "Well, I guess that's why they call it a vacation. J.-M. would like a vacation, wouldn't you Jean-Marie? A vacation? Don't we both need a holiday?"

(I'd missed the beginning of that bit of conversation, watching Jean-Marie.)

Zipporah smiled vaguely my way as the others laughed cutely, the dog getting me full-on.

When the two were inside and we could hear their rumbles on the stairs, dog tags jingling, Gloria with her voice lowered said, "I've never found her anything but snooty—just personally."

"I like her," said Steven, agitating the vehicle. "But yeah, the Frenchness."

"Israeli," Gloria provided slyly.

It was as though a stranger had dared to fart boisterously in new company, just trying out the waters. Melissa stood up with her empty glass, aimed a cheek at the ceiling, and whispered, "She ought to be up there by now. Yep. I hear the door. Who'd like another? Steven, Gloria?"

Gloria said that she expected she was ready to go lie down for a little while.

She raised her voice saying this, addressing everyone generally. Still, she didn't move.

Steven's head bobbed downward and downward, and he burbled, "I'm ready for another cold one, honey."

My face caught a glint of distraction just as a text came in from Perry.

Hi there!

Hearing from him always set off another kind of Pavlovian response in me. I likened it to a nursing mother whose milk began to run at the sound of her infant's cry. I texted back:

How are you?

He wasted no time.

When are you coming home again!

Perry favored the exclamation point.

At the end of the month

I had a habit of not putting the period at the end of my last sentence or phrase. I wasn't trying to be cute or stylish. I was just caught up in the current electronic-communication mode of exploiting the rapidity texting allowed. I'd never liked talking on the phone, not since I was a teen trying to convince a girl I was indeed for her, quite heterosexual, and, yes, certainly straight enough to satisfy her need to be listened to and understood for hours. Having told so many lies over the phone as a would-be adolescent swain, then, I hardly trusted my speaking voice, and it was only a decade and a half later, when I was a Peace Corps volunteer in a very small town in the Czech Republic teaching English as a second language, that I began to regain some of my phone chops talking long-distance to Perry, who lived in Paris, where we'd met. AIDS had destroyed my sex life and had long threatened my sense of romance. If I could divide sex and romance I was gold, so I'd hit my sweet spot on the one hand with the understanding Perry, and on the other with my anonymous encounters before mostly stopping having those as I got older. Perry only expected me to be there physically or else just in touch, available, which made him more modern than me. He was more modern than me in most ways. He'd taught me I could have virtually everything I desired—as long as I understood what sacrifices to others' happiness and comfort I was making. I had watched him making this dizzying social calculus with old friends and colleagues and new younger lovers when he was still taking those. He'd loved many younger men who crawled back in time, enthralled by his gradually developing fame. He wasn't a Harold Robbins, Stephen King, or Danielle Steel. His notoriety never receded but grew like a baby blue-chip stock. Now his health was faltering again, and I wondered if not for all time this go-round. I loved him because I'd originally believed in him long before we'd ever met when no one else I knew had read him and I was the sole stander on that shore, doing a vigil on a dark mystical night. But I also loved him because with him it was an automatic response. He had an innocence, loving whom he loved. I deserved none of his generosity, or at least I hadn't begun to earn it until recently.

That long? Beau says hi!

My first affair outside of the relationship, besides the threesome and foursome sex scenes Perry and I had gotten into in Paris, had been with the much younger Beau. Beau had come to us as a fan of Perry's, having just moved to New York from Princeton. He was an architect working for a construction company that threw up mile-high mega-Manhattan apartment towers wherever investors and developers could get traction, meaning were able to bend the old laws, kick out the current tenants, and tear down their existing domiciles. Beau was rakishly bitter. Tightly knit, as Perry liked to say, Beau knew he was short but had minded his figure from a young age when his ex-navy father had taught him to do morning calisthenics. His torso was flat, neat with squarely articulated abdominals. Subtly he dressed this physique nattily in Uniqlo, that Japanese Gap. Had he lived in the time of *Brideshead Revisited,* Beau would have fit in convincingly, with his Marxist notions of capitalism, while posing either as the scion of landed gentry or one of their hangers-on. He hated his employers, really hated the modern world despite his iPhone and the iPad on which he read his Swinburne, Pater, and Ruskin free, or else for 99 cents. *Blue blue wretched blue.* We lay in bed in the apartment and could not figure out a reason to continue. I wasn't surprised, but I was in love and that's the hell of an open relationship: you're already taken, which is a fancier, more dignified version of damaged goods. Oh, how I preferred promiscuity, meaningless hook-ups started in bars, and Key West was the ground zero of these activities for me. The island was my trigger, the way to fire an oblivious bullet of caring not at all, of not worrying but letting the night take me. Throughout the year in New York, where more and more sexual encounters happened over cell phones, I saved up my slutty sex points and redeemed them in Key West. (As I'd written in Chapter Two of *The Husband,* I preferred to take my chances in person with a suitor; photos didn't show me in my most advantageous light.) But I was also getting older, and in my memoir—in a taking-stock sort of way, as though I were waving bye-bye to a lifestyle I'd never quite mastered—I wanted to show that I was a reasonable person, someone who could be funny, since wasn't gay life funny, not really that threatening, in the final analysis, right?—no, in *The Husband* I wanted to entertain newly. To disarm, to tell straight people who felt threatened somehow by the recent freedoms gay people enjoyed thanks to the Supreme Court and other local protections and ordinances that gay life was mostly ordinary. I was trying to make my life comical, the stuff of smiles, because of its banality. This may have been my first mistake.

If his gossip was to be believed, Truman Capote once wrote about the time he'd met E. M. Forster, who incredibly was two full generations older than Capote. Forster had told him that as a young man he'd always hoped as he got older his libido would calm down, so that gradually he would feel less and less yearnful, but it had never happened. Going into his nineties, Forster had thought about sex constantly. Recalling the anecdote, I felt hungry and left Ham's guesthouse to find something quick and good to eat, telling myself I probably wouldn't then slip into one of the bars while I was downtown, conveniently, so to speak. But as usual I doubted my own resolve. I wanted to stay slim, which was already past as a condition or feature, but I told myself to satisfy my yens. I ended up sitting on a curb on Duval eating a slice of pizza. When that wasn't enough I went next door and got a three-pack of fried chicken with a side of coleslaw and a roll.

HE PUTS ON warm fuzzy wool socks. There's supposed to be snow tomorrow and Perry can feel a chill edging into the poorly glazed windows and gathering force with every outside gust, sluicing in foot-level drafts along the wall-to-wall carpet's surface. It excites him. He's remembering the winters of Ohio and Illinois when he was a kid, and the winters that bit into the suit he bought on time to look presentable and professional as a young journalist when he first moved to New York in the sixties, not actually wanting to be a journalist any more than he wanted to be a businessman (what his father wanted him to be). The cold is a cozy reminder of sacrifices he made. If his father was ever proud of him, the man never said. Now Perry's the age the old man was when he died eating from a TV tray in front of the evening news in Cincinnati, dead sitting up, Perry's stepmother said, eyes still open in front of Jimmy Carter, whom he loathed and loved loathing, she also said, so that his father wouldn't miss a minute of the cracker's grin on his RCA screen for the life of him. The old man had lived in a mock Tudor that contained numerous useless and unused rooms, and Perry by then had been living in a roach trap of an apartment on Lafayette, carrying on with his sex-obsessed life and finishing freelance projects so that he could get back to the novel about his tortured adolescence beneath this bastard's gaze.

Now Perry sometimes felt, having retired from teaching at venerable Princeton, that he was sleeping through his rising and walking days, padding around on the comfy carpet of the Chelsea apartment (he was worth more dead to some than alive, and it made him grin, living in nearly two million dollars' worth of Manhattan real estate bought a long time ago for a fraction of what, when global uncertainty and terrorism had knocked the breath out of the market, he'd bought it for). He was dozy. He felt cozy summing up this life in a new book, with his recent prize, a life that, although he hadn't ever hit any bestseller list, had been interesting and affected others' lives. Plus, he'd had his fun. Since his heart attack he'd stabilized and felt fresh with new arteries in his left ventricle; felt that he could go on for a time. He slept a lot and was sleepy the first half of the day. He was okay. Could bathe himself without incident or near-incident, could call the pharmacy for delivery of his meds, could order anything in this ordering-out city.

Might only see a delivery boy in an entire day other than faithful Beau, who's leaving for the evening, and who says, "Perry, honey? I feel like I need to go but I'll be back by eleven . . ."

Beau's having dinner with colleagues from his department. Beau's quick and moves with a supple accuracy. Youth is like that. It's okay that Scott is gone so long as he has Beau as a kind, conscientious caregiver. Beau is beautiful, the collegiate equivalent of Perry's lost, anxious prep school years. He instant-broils Perry's ribeye and heats creamed spinach expensively purchased in a plastic tub from the gourmet shop across the street where Perry lunches and goes over for his skinny lattes when he's being interviewed, and it's all fine, it's dearly bought—and he's alive.

"I shouldn't be later than eleven," repeats Beau and kisses Perry's cheek heading out.

He'd forgotten his solitude, the délice of ignoring and half-contemplating a project as he moved about in his roach trap on Lafayette. Of expecting a midnight dalliance and of having his whole future ahead of him, long over-the-horizon stretches of future success and of happiness, which he supposes he's accomplished—as much as he ever would, Perry hazards. He sometimes forgets the groaning, gnawing inner doubts. But those have only added to his legend.

He sits at the dining table, the only set of furniture Scott has brought to the household.

He has a man, one who always comes home but ventures out in wider and wider circles as Perry, comfortably cared for, enjoying his aloneness, waits like a sea wife, the captain's lady. He himself once adventured, but now he's married to the adventurer. He's contented, comfortably confused.

Dimness, like a mental lack, is beginning to engulf him, he fears. He's losing all time.

DOES PERRY REMEMBER Jakob, who for a time was my younger, second lover? Shown a photo, he would surely remember Jakob's face. Although I wonder now if Jakob's name would come readily to Perry's mind. Jakob and I lived, except for the first two months in New York, in separate cities. I went heavily into debt flying to see him. He was down south finishing his PhD. He was up in Boston on his postdoctoral fellowship. He was spending the summer, every summer, in Munich with his family—those international flights, and I was never organized enough to record and add up miles to apply to later flights. And though I loved him, keeping up with Jakob became a dare for me: How far could I take myself into the red, which my father would find shocking (even as I never shared details of my debt with my father)? Like many gay men, I was running from those constrictions, flouting them privately, telling myself . . . what? I was living the life no one in my family had ever had the curiosity to live—I won't call it courage. But with Jakob (and Perry, for a time the three of us being a trio, although never in bed), I was seeing the Greek islands, the South of France, London, Rome, Berlin. We tried to see every city in Germany and Austria, those he'd seen but wanted to show me and those he'd never seen. It was never perfect but we stuck. It was work, then it wasn't. It was long conversations, then some full days of telephone silence. We argued, at elections, or on the why and how of fooling around separately. I had told him early on, "I don't want you coming back to me later and saying you wasted the best years of your life on me. Go out and fool around, have fun. I want you to fool around and have fun." But this was really because I feared my own roaming. And getting old, probably, although not so much. I always knew aging was in the offing, sooner for me than him.

Now here I am, a middle-aged man in a dry season not promising cool rain. Without Jakob, and wondering. One of our last snapshots: in Heidelberg taking the Philosophers' Walk—during one of our last months of freedom together before things changed. The day was hot, but we took bottles of water crossing the forceful Neckar. These hikes, these treks not in silence, exactly, but only occasionally speaking, the gray-green Neckar flowing on, and, as always, I was preoccupied. We stopped at the top of a hill overlooking the river, still not talking about Perry. Perry was in a mental holding pattern of ours, no longer intruding on my time with Jakob, but still I thought about Perry—my little sin. Perry was always there, like a parent, like a beloved sibling. Later I had stopped feeling guilty about Perry, and Jakob had stopped correcting me for bringing him up. We'd reached a peace, a final perfection, so that we could be together, just be together and enjoy our time, knowing we'd soon part and go back to our separate other places.

Now Jakob's in Pittsburgh, and things have changed indeed. We're no longer together.

I USED TO think of death like an enemy, but not anymore. Death was like loneliness, then loneliness became a comfort. Now that I'm totally alone, Perry gone, Jakob gone, I romanticize the dark spaces. The apartment in New York is paces of cozy aloneness. When Perry was alive, he used to say, "I want to make sure you can stay here." He frowned approvingly at me and then he bent down at paperwork trying to make sense of it—it was already long neatly tied-up. It was straightforward, not needing his further attention, but still he worried, the disease of aging, losing his hold, haranguing him vaguely, even comfortably, until maybe he'd miss his footing and fall.

I recently heard from Jakob, who called and said, "I've met somebody who's really nice."

It had been months since we'd talked and I said, "Hey, that's wonderful."

"I was hoping you'd say that. Actually, you'd say that. How are you? Are you okay?"

"I'm okay. What's he like?"

"He's really wonderful. He's an academic, too."

"Well, that's perfect. Tell me about him."

I heard him sigh and waited, and then he said, "He's beautiful and I don't deserve him."

"History of gay life."

"Right?"

"Are you happy?"

"I think I am."

"Then that's everything."

And we talked for upwards of an hour.

I never sold that memoir, *The Husband*. No one would want it, Stella finally decided.

She spoke of regrets, but, ultimately, I decided it was the one book I had to write but didn't necessarily have to publish.

I remember a kid I'd known for an hour and a half in my room in Ham's guesthouse, who, stoned and sensual and physically half-deep into me, said, "It's not about us, you know? It's about the rest of the world. We're just here, looking at things from over here. You know? We're just hydrogen . . ."

Acknowledgments

Ruth Greenstein has been everything from beginning to end, hands-on, maybe a little indulgent but also inspiring, at times tough, at other times felicitously querying. Ruth, I feel you picked me out from a crowd of hopeful gazes, and I'm grateful. I would not have had this second book without you.

To Edmund White, my husband, and Giuseppe Gullo, Little Brother.

To Jeff Bond, my great friend, who read many of these pages in their earliest forms.

Philipp Stelzel, contained in this book, with love for the space and light to work in your company, and with so much affection over thirteen years and beyond. And to your family.

David McConnell and Darrell Crawford, for your shelter and friendship and love.

Patrick Merla, an early boost, there from almost the very beginning.

Ann Beattie and Lincoln Perry, thank you.

Alison Lurie and Edward Hower, for so much.

Joy Williams.

Ryan Runstadler.

Joyce Carol Oates and Charles Gross.

Sheila Kohler and Bill Tucker.

Alden Jones: our friendship.

Joshua Forsyth, Richard Wilde Lopez, Joshua Gustwiller, and Ryan Ostrowski from Barracuda.

Michael Davis.

To my colleagues at John Cabot University in Rome, Carlos Dews, Elizabeth Geoghegan, Susan Bradley Smith, as well as to my students there.

Neel Mukherjee, thank you.

Christopher Witte and your parents, Paulette and Eric—thank you.

Brian Alessandro and Sam and Sean Desmond and Lupe Rodarte and Tom Scutro.

Stuart Waterman.

To the memory of Raymond Smith and to the memory of George Pitcher.

To the memory of Sandy McClatchy.

And finally to Xan Price, for your friendship.